He Shouldn't Be Kissing Lucy...

his assistant, his friend, the one person he didn't want to offend because, as he often joked, she knew where the bodies were buried.

But she felt good. She smelled good. And she tasted amazing.

Since puberty, he'd had his share of fantasies. But no dream, no matter how erotic, could ever live up to what was happening right here, right now.

If they didn't stop soon, it would be too late.

But he had no intention of stopping. The ground would have to open up and swallow him whole. This elevator that had trapped them so securely would have to break from its cables and crush them like pancakes. Because unless an act of God pulled them apart, he was going to make love to Lucy Grainger.

Finally.

Dear Reader,

Thank you for choosing Silhouette Desire, where this month we have six fabulous novels for you to enjoy. We start things off with *Estate Affair* by Sara Orwig, the latest installment of the continuing DYNASTIES: THE ASHTONS series. In this upstairs/downstairs-themed story, the Ashtons' maid falls for an Ashton son and all sorts of scandal follows. And in Maureen Child's *Whatever Reilly Wants…*, the second title in the THREE-WAY WAGER series, a sexy marine gets an unexpected surprise when he falls for his suddenly transformed gal pal.

Susan Crosby concludes her BEHIND CLOSED DOORS series with *Secrets of Paternity*. The secret baby in this book just happens to be eighteen years old…. Hmm, there's quite the story behind that revelation. The wonderful Emilie Rose presents *Scandalous Passion,* a sultry tale of a woman desperate to get back some steamy photos from her past lover. Of course, he has a price for returning those pictures, but it's not money he's after. *The Sultan's Bed,* by Laura Wright, continues the tales of her sheikh heroes with an enigmatic male who is searching for his missing sister and finds a startling attraction to her lovely neighbor. And finally, what was supposed to be just an elevator ride turns into a very passionate encounter, in *Blame It on the Blackout* by Heidi Betts.

Sit back and enjoy all of the smart, sensual stories Silhouette Desire has to offer.

Happy reading,

Melissa Jeglinski

Melissa Jeglinski
Senior Editor
Silhouette Desire

Please address questions and book requests to:
Silhouette Reader Service
U.S.: 3010 Walden Ave., P.O. Box 1325, Buffalo, NY 14269
Canadian: P.O. Box 609, Fort Erie, Ont. L2A 5X3

Blame It on the Blackout

HEIDI BETTS

Published by Silhouette Books

America's Publisher of Contemporary Romance

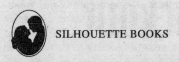 **SILHOUETTE BOOKS**

ISBN 0-373-76662-9

BLAME IT ON THE BLACKOUT

Visit Silhouette Books at www.eHarlequin.com

Printed in U.S.A.

Books by Heidi Betts

Silhouette Desire

Bought by a Millionaire #1638
Blame It on the Blackout #1662

HEIDI BETTS

An avid romance reader since junior high school, Heidi knew early on that she wanted to write these wonderful stories of love and adventure. It wasn't until her freshman year of college, however, when she spent the entire night reading a romance novel instead of studying for finals, that she decided to take the road less traveled and follow her dream. In addition to reading, writing and romance, she is the founder of her local Romance Writers of America chapter and has a tendency to take injured and homeless animals of every species into her central Pennsylvania home.

Heidi loves to hear from readers. You can write to her at P.O. Box 99, Kylertown, PA 16847 (a SASE is appreciated but not necessary), or e-mail heidi@heidibetts.com. And be sure to visit www.heidibetts.com for news and information about upcoming books.

To Maureen Child and Leanne Banks—

Friends and fellow Desire authors,
you've inspired me more than you can ever know.
Thank you for your wonderful stories that remind me of
why I love this line so much, and for all the great advice
you've offered this past year.

And to my Absolutely Fabulous editor,
Melissa Jeglinski—Thank you for taking me under
your wing, teaching me the ins and outs of the
Desire line and making me love what I'm writing
even more than I did to begin with.

With many thanks to fellow WRW member
Sandy Rangel for her help with the research for this book
and willingness to share her firsthand knowledge
of the Georgetown area.

And always, for Daddy.

One

Lucy Grainger tapped softly in warning on the front door of Peter Reynolds's town house, then used a key to let herself in. Gathering the morning mail and paper from the foyer floor, she made her way past the den that held her office to the large kitchen at the back of the house. Setting the paper and mail alongside her purse on the island countertop, she started a pot of coffee and began clearing away some of last night's mess.

It wasn't her job to clean up after Peter. He did have a housekeeper, after all, who dropped by once a week to do laundry and dishes and relocate some of the dust that settled on miscellaneous surfaces. But Lucy was so used to taking care of him that it seemed only natural to move a few dirty dishes to the sink or throw away a near-empty carton of milk that had been left out of the refrigerator too long.

From there, she walked back toward the front of the house, up the stairs, and down the short hallway that led to Peter's bedroom. He might have slept in, especially if he'd been up late working on some computer program or another. Or maybe he'd simply forgotten to set his alarm clock—again. But his bed was empty, the sheets tangled and nearly stripped off the mattress.

Only one place left to look. Lucy eased the bedroom door closed and walked across the hallway in the opposite direction to Peter's home office.

Less conservative than the den, Peter liked this room because it was small, private, and casually decorated to his personal tastes. Which basically meant unadorned walls painted periwinkle-blue with white trim, a three-part desk taking up one whole corner, and low tables of sliding file drawers lining the remaining three. Every available surface was filled with assorted computer equipment, ongoing work projects, and Peter's collection of original *Star Trek* action figures.

Inside, the computer tower hummed softly from its home on the floor, telling her she was right about Peter's location. With one arm folded beneath his head, Lucy's boss slept hunched over his cluttered desk. He wore an old gray T-shirt and plaid boxers, his sandy-blond hair ruffled and sticking up in places—probably from all the times he'd run his fingers through it in frustration during the night.

Lucy's own fingers clenched at her sides as she fought the urge to flatten those spiky spots or slide a palm down the strong curve of his spine.

She sighed. This was the problem with working for a man she had half a crush on. The line between employer and potential lover got blurrier by the day.

But only for her. Peter didn't see her as potential lover material. Most of the time, she didn't think he saw her as a woman at all.

As a secretary, an assistant, the person he ran to when he needed just about anything, yes. But as an attractive, interested, flesh-and-blood woman? He'd never glanced up from his computer screen long enough to notice.

Then again, that was one of the things she loved about him—his passion for software design and starting his own company from the ground up. He was brilliant and already had corporations from around the world calling him to help work bugs out of their systems or simply get things running more smoothly. But what he loved most was designing his own games and programs, and that had been his focus for the past two years, ever since she'd started working for him.

Reaching past his sleeping form, she collected several empty cola cans scattered over the desktop and on the floor. He drank too much of this syrupy stuff, especially when he was busy and became nearly obsessed with a particular project.

Two of the aluminum cans slipped from her grasp and rattled as they bounced against each other on the way to the carpeted floor. The noise startled Peter and he shot upright. Blinking sleepily, he looked around as though he wasn't quite sure where he was.

"I'm sorry," Lucy said softly. "I didn't mean to wake you."

He rubbed a hand across his eyes and yawned. "What time is it?"

"A little past nine. How long have you been working?"

"I started after dinner. Around six, I guess."

Pushing back his chair, he got to his feet and stretched. His knuckles nearly grazed the ceiling as he raised his arms high above his head and stood on tiptoe. The posture puffed out his chest and showed the taut, well-defined muscles of his calves and thighs.

A ripple of awareness shot through Lucy, but she pretended not to notice.

"I was working on that GlobalCon glitch. It took me longer than I expected, but I think I took care of the problem."

She moved to the wastebasket near the door and dumped the soda cans in, making a mental note to recycle them later. "So those were billable hours you spent last night. What time did you finish?"

"Damned if I know." He scratched a spot on his chest and yawned again. "The last time I remember looking at the clock, it was about 3:00 a.m."

She nodded, wondering if GlobalCon and all of Peter's other clients realized just what a bargain they usually got with him. Sure, he was expensive, but he was also the best. And since he rarely remembered to log the times he began and ended his work for them, the bills she sent were generally best-guess estimates.

"Why don't you go lie down for a couple of hours. You look exhausted."

The grin he shot her swept right down to her toes and curled them inside her plain navy pumps.

"Nah. Now that I'm up, I might as well get showered and dressed."

Peter in the shower. Now there was an image she needed floating around her brain the rest of the morning. As though he didn't already keep her wide-awake most nights.

"Besides, I want to call GlobalCon and let them know I took care of their problem, then see if I can make any more progress on Soldiers of Misfortune."

Soldiers of Misfortune was Peter's latest obsession, a virtual guerilla warfare game with enough blood and guts to keep adolescent boys entranced for hours. Lucy tried to work up a modicum of outrage for his perpetuation of teen violence, but she played the games herself from time to time and had to admit they were fun. And so far, she hadn't snapped and committed any acts of mass destruction.

Careful not to touch him, she moved around the office, collecting the rest of the clutter from Peter's long work night. "Don't forget to try on your tux and see if it needs alterations before tomorrow night."

Halfway out the door, he froze. Twisting his neck just far enough to look at her, he asked, "What's tomorrow night?"

"The City Women benefit against domestic violence. You're giving a speech and receiving an award for your support of the organization and donations of refurbished computers to local battered women's shelters."

He'd spent weeks upgrading old systems so women who were trying to escape unbearable situations could train for new jobs to support themselves and their children instead of feeling forced to return to abusive husbands.

His eyes closed, chin dropping to his chest. "Damn, I forgot. I don't suppose there's any way I can get out of it," he said, shooting her a hopeful expression.

She bit down on a smile, not wanting to encourage him. "Not unless you want to disappoint hundreds of grateful women and children."

With a sigh, he rested his hands on his hips. "Fine. But I'm going to need a date."

A stab of pain hit her low in the belly. Followed quickly by envy and regret.

Peter had dated hordes of beautiful, successful ladies. Models, actresses, news anchors, real estate agents… He was handsome, funny, charming, and—though he was still striving to build his software company into one that would rival the best of the best—wealthy enough to catch a single girl's attention.

Lucy told herself it didn't hurt to see him with all those other women. Except when she came to work in the morning and discovered them still in his bed, or just leaving, or found a stray pair of panties while cleaning up between the housekeeper's visits.

"I'll go through your Rolodex and see who might be available."

A minute ticked by while Peter stood in the doorway and she lifted the now-full plastic bag from the metal trash can.

"No," he said, startling her. "I don't feel like putting on a show for someone who just wants to be seen with the great Peter Reynolds."

"That's all right. I'm sure the City Women will understand if you attend alone."

"I have a better idea," he announced, turning around to face her. "You can come with me instead."

He said it as though he'd decided to have chicken for dinner over steak, and Lucy couldn't help but feel like the feathered creature unfortunate enough to be dragged to the chopping block.

If he'd meant it as a real invitation, if he'd even once looked at her as though he wanted her on his arm for the evening because he was attracted to her, she might have considered it.

Oh, who was she kidding? She'd have jumped at the chance and prayed he didn't lose interest before the main course.

Shaking her head, she gathered the edges of the garbage bag together to keep the items from falling out and headed for the stairs, brushing past him with barely a millimeter of space to spare. "No, thank you."

"No? What do you mean *no?*"

His voice, raised in surprised indignation, followed her down the steps. As she rounded the newel post and headed for the kitchen, she noticed he was hot on her heels.

"Lucy, you can't possibly mean to leave me to my own devices. I'll drown in a sea of shiny, happy people. You know how much I hate crowds and public speaking."

"You should have thought of that before you agreed to be there." She set the trash from his office on the countertop and began separating it into the plastic recycling bins set in one corner.

"God, that coffee smells good," he murmured, tossing a longing glance at the pot that had just finished dripping. "Look, I can't go alone. I *need* you with me. There are going to be some very important people in attendance. People who could turn into future clients or help get Reyware and Games of PRey off the ground. You're my assistant. You know our software programs and intentions for the company almost as well as I do. And no one works a room like you do. People love you."

When she didn't respond, he continued, sounding more desperate by the second. "Consider it in your job description. I'll pay you overtime. You can take the appointment book and set up a dozen meetings with potential backers for the next month."

Ah, yes. She was, indeed, his assistant. And if he was making this into a work-related affair, then she had no choice but to go with him.

But she didn't have to make it easy for him.

Turning from the recycle bins, she leaned back against the counter and crossed her arms beneath her breasts. "You won't be so impressed when I show up in jeans and a ratty sweatshirt. I don't have anything appropriate to wear to a high-priced charity dinner."

Relief washed over Peter's features and he slapped his hands down flat on the marble island as the corners of his mouth turned up in a grin. "Not a problem. I'll take care of everything. Or rather, you'll take care of everything, but I'll foot the bill. Here…"

He reached back, as though digging into a hip pocket, then realized he was still in his boxers. Shaking his head, he rushed to assure her. "Don't worry, I'll get you a credit card. I'll get you two credit cards. Buy whatever you want."

Then he came around the island, reached her in three long strides, and wrapped her in a hug tight enough to crush her ribcage. "Thank you, thank you, thank you." He punctuated each adulation with a kiss to her temple.

Lucy's knees grew weak and she let her eyes drift shut as the heat of his body seeped through the thin material of her white blouse, short navy skirt and stockings.

Oh, sure. She could spend the evening with this man and remember it was nothing but business. No problem. And maybe after performing that small miracle, she'd practice turning water into wine.

Peter slugged back his sixth cup of coffee since Lucy had awakened him this morning and punched the computer mouse to send the cache of e-mails he'd composed in the last half hour.

He was learning that it wasn't easy taking care of himself. She'd only been gone two and a half hours, but she was usually around during the day to answer the phone and come when he called, so he was finding it difficult to carry out his normal routine.

He'd finally given up answering the telephone when it rang every five minutes, and was now letting all calls go directly to voicemail. Lord knew Lucy would be better able to deal with the messages when she got back. And even though she often went through his electronic mail for him, forwarding only those that required his personal attention, today he'd done it himself. He wasn't completely helpless, after all.

The snail mail, however, was a different matter. No way was he going anywhere near that pile of paper cuts. Lucy would let him know if there was anything he needed to see.

From his office upstairs, he heard the front door open and a wash of relief poured over him. Thank God. Now he could lock himself in his room and concentrate on his real strength—program design—instead of dealing with the other odds and ends of getting through the day.

Crossing his office threshold, he stopped on the second floor landing and watched as Lucy struggled to close the door while balancing assorted shopping bags and boxes in both arms.

Looking up, she spotted him and blew a stray strand of straight black hair out of her face. "You could offer to help, you know."

"Oh. Right." He spent more time with computers than people, and Lucy would be the first to point out that he sometimes lacked social graces. But the minute she called him on it, he rushed into action, bounding down the stairs and grabbing up her entire load.

"Sorry about that. It looks like you had luck shopping, anyway."

She shrugged out of the lightweight jacket that matched her dark blue skirt, tossing it over the banister and leaving her once again in a soft white blouse that showed off her feminine attributes to perfection. It didn't help that he could see the outline of her black lace bra through the gauzy material, either.

Peter's blood thickened and a lump of temptation formed in his throat. But a moment later, he tamped down on both, refusing to let his mind wander a path he had no business exploring.

Lucy was a beauty, no doubt about it. From the moment they'd met, when she'd first interviewed for the job as his personal assistant, he'd been fascinated by the silky fall of her long ebony hair, the smooth complexion of her porcelain skin, the bright, sharp blue of her doe-shaped eyes.

Of course, there was no chance of anything happening between them. Peter had long ago put a mental block on the possibility of building a relationship with any woman, let alone one who worked for him. God forbid he turn out like his father…. He had too much in common with the old man already and had no intention of making a wife or children as miserable as his father had made his mother and him.

But he'd hired Lucy in spite of his attraction to her, simply because she was the best damn applicant on the list. She typed, took dictation, had a phone voice that could make a saint fall to his knees, and knew her way around computers almost as well as he did.

So, if he found himself staring at her ripe red lips most of the time while she spoke, or taking an unnatural number of cold showers after she'd gone home for the day, he had no one to blame but himself.

Dressed now in a clean pair of tan chinos and dark green polo shirt, he noticed the curve of her mouth and wondered what she found so amusing. Lord knew he was in too much physical pain to mimic her contented smile.

"I hope you still think it was a good idea to make me go with you tomorrow night once you see your credit card statement."

That gave him a moment's pause, but then he shrugged. The tissue paper in several of the boutique bags rustled with the movement. "How bad could it be?"

Her brows shot up. Holding a hand out like she expected him to shake it, she quipped, "Hi, let me introduce myself. I'm a woman with *carte blanche* to charge anything I want on a man's account. I also happen to know your net worth. Any questions?"

He chuckled. Her sense of humor had always been machete sharp, but that was just one more reason he enjoyed her company.

"Remind me to have a couple of drinks before I open the bill," he returned. "In the meantime, how about a little fashion show?"

Eyes wide, she shook her head. "I don't think so."

"Come on," he cajoled. "I want to see what I paid for."

Furry, multilegged caterpillars wiggled inside Lucy's stomach as she considered Peter's request. The last thing she wanted to do was attend tomorrow night's charity benefit with him, and the next to the last thing she wanted was to model her new evening gown before she absolutely had to.

But—whether he knew it yet or not—he had spent quite a lot on the fancy ensemble, and if he wanted an advance viewing, she supposed it was only right to give it to him.

He must have read the indecision on her face because

he started up the stairs without her. "You can use my bedroom to change. And this way, I'll know what color corsage to order."

"Corsage?" With a roll of her eyes, she began to follow. "Peter, we aren't going to a high school prom."

He swung around at the balcony railing and flashed her the unwitting, thousand-watt smile that made her teeth sweat. "Too bad. It sure would be more fun than what we have to endure." Then he spun back and walked into the bedroom.

When Lucy arrived, the bags and boxes he'd carried up for her were scattered atop the chest at the foot of his bed. Peter rubbed his hands together and gave her a friendly wink before moving back toward the hallway.

"Give me a yell when you're ready. I'll be in my office."

The door closed with a soft click, leaving her alone beside Peter's bed…and Peter's mattress…and Peter's pillow. The covers were still rumpled from the last time he'd slept there and it took a great deal of effort not to throw herself across the bed and inhale his scent from every fiber of the tan, five hundred thread count Egyptian cotton sheets. She ought to know, she'd bought them for him.

Sad, that's what she was. Pathetic and sad and unworthy of being a member of the female race. What other twenty-nine-year-old woman spent her life mooning over an unattainable boss? A clueless man who never looked twice at her…at least not the way a man should look at a woman.

Other than throwing herself down on his desk and screaming, "Take me, big boy!" she'd done everything she could think of to let Peter know she was interested. From the time she'd started working for him two years ago, she'd tried to drop hints that his advances wouldn't be unwelcome. She'd worn her skirts a little short and her blouses a little low. She'd worn a dozen different perfumes, trying to find one that would pique his interest. She'd worn her hair up and down, short and long, straight, curly, braided…She'd leaned close while they talked and fabricated excuses to interrupt him while he worked.

Finally, when nothing seemed to catch his attention, she'd given up. A girl could only take so much humiliation, and her breaking point came the day she'd arrived at work to find another woman, half-dressed, leaving Peter's room. Her theory that he must be gay had been shot all to hell, and she'd vowed then and there never to make another move on him.

Unfortunately that pledge didn't keep her eyes from wandering over his well-muscled form, or her heart from skipping a beat when he said her name in that low, reverberating voice of his.

Not for the first time, she thought about quitting. She really should. She was talented, good at her job, and could probably find another position anywhere in the city within the week.

But she liked this arrangement. Despite the personal misery she suffered on a daily basis, Peter was a great employer. She believed in what he was doing and enjoyed being a part of it.

Besides, what other boss would spring for a gorgeous new evening gown and accessories that she would probably never have occasion to wear again?

Lifting items from their bags, she began to peel out of her practical skirt and blouse, ignoring the skittering of awareness that skated down her spine when she realized she was standing half-naked in the middle of Peter's bedroom. If only he were here with her, and she was stripping down to her skin for something other than an impromptu fashion show.

Instead of bothering with the fancy undergarments she'd purchased to go with the dress, she remained in her normal bra and panty hose, and simply slipped the gown on overtop. She did trade her plain pumps for the black, glitter-covered velvet stilettos, though.

Sweeping her hair back off her shoulders, she left the bedroom and crossed the short, carpeted hall to Peter's office. She stopped in the doorway, leaned casually against the frame and watched his fingers fly over the keyboard.

"So," she said, catching his attention. "What do you think?"

Two

Peter glanced up from the computer screen, wondering why she hadn't called for him when she was finished. He'd have gone over to the bedroom to see her new dress instead of making her come all the way over here.

And then his brain stopped functioning altogether. Every thought in his head flew out his ears as he stared at the vision before him.

He slid the wire-rim glasses from his nose to get a better look, but she still looked stunningly beautiful. Her hair fell about her face in an ebony curtain and the red satin of her gown, overlaid with black velvet in an intricate flowered pattern, brought out the rosy tint of her alabaster skin.

And that was just from the neck up. From the neck down, she made his eyes sting, his mouth go dry and his nerve endings sizzle.

He'd always known Lucy had a fabulous body. All the straight skirts and tailored jackets in the world couldn't hide that. But this dress, with its spaghetti straps and scallop-edged bodice, high-slit skirt and the three to four inch heels that made her legs go on for eternity, brought out every nuance of her drop-dead figure.

His gaze drifted over the generous swell of her breasts, the slim line of her waist, the gentle curve of her hips, and up again. Her ice-blue eyes met his and for the first time in his life, he found himself at a loss for words. Speechless, when he'd thought that was something only movie stars suffered because a script called for it.

After several long seconds of complete, utter silence, Lucy interrupted his total lack of thought and started blood flowing back to his brain.

"What?" she asked, glancing down at herself as though something was wrong with the awe-inspiring concoction she was wearing. "Don't you like it? Should I take it back?"

"No!" he yelped, too fast and too loud. Taking a breath, he tempered his tone and added, "It's perfect. I was just…" *Admiring the view…thinking sinful thoughts…looking for a way to get you out of it…* "Thinking of all the heads you're going to turn tomorrow night. We may have to beat men off with a stick."

Her cheeks colored prettily and she lowered her eyes for a moment. "Thank you."

"You won't have any trouble stirring up interest for Reyware in that outfit."

He regretted the words as soon as they left his mouth. What was he thinking, effectively equating her attending the charity soiree in that dress to prostitution? *Hey, Luce, how about fixing yourself up and coming to dinner with me so you can give new meaning to "pressing the flesh" and drum up a little financial support for my personal corporation?*

Lord, he felt like a pimp.

And he knew his comment hurt her because she lowered her head and traced invisible designs on the carpet with the toe of her shoe.

Scrubbing a hand over his face, he cursed silently. "That didn't come out right," he tried to apologize.

She raised her eyes to his, dark and shadowed, and offered a weak smile. "I know what you meant."

No, she didn't, but he couldn't think of a way to further explain himself without making matters worse.

"I'd better go change back," she said, letting her gaze slide away from him again. "Before I get stained or torn or wrinkled."

He could think of a couple of things he wouldn't mind doing to tear or wrinkle her gown. And he'd happily pay for another when they were finished.

As quickly as that image entered his mind, he shut it down. Lucy turned, heading back to his bedroom, and there was enough testosterone swimming around in his veins at the moment to watch her walk away and enjoy every elegant, long-legged stride.

But that was as far as it could go—watching. Lucy wasn't one of the women who snuggled up to him at parties and made it clear they were hoping to spend the night in his bed.

As much as he might wish differently, he couldn't use her to scratch this itch that was suddenly driving him crazy. She was his assistant, and he hoped a friend. Those were two things he wasn't willing to risk.

Worse than that, though, Lucy wasn't a woman he could walk away from in the morning. She would always be here, working for him, helping him to market his software designs and computer know-how, and filling the holes in his own personality with her award-winning people skills.

Dropping into his desk chair, he sent it spinning and watched the blue of the walls swirl around him. What a mess. He should have hired a man to answer the phone and open his mail. He sure as hell wouldn't be having this problem then.

But Lucy was the best, and he honestly wouldn't want to work with anyone else, no matter how hard it was to ignore her presence.

If he started something with Lucy, there would be no one-night stand, no casual roll in the hay that could be forgotten and ignored ten minutes later. She wasn't that kind of girl.

And if she wasn't *that* kind of girl, then she was the other. The forever kind, with visions of marriage and children and picket fences dancing in her brain.

That kind scared Peter to death. He'd decided long ago never to let a personal, romantic relationship cloud his acumen for business.

His father had tried to have both and failed miserably. Oh, his company was a smashing success, but his marriage might as well have been a house afire. He'd spent all his time at the office, put all of his energy into deals and negotiations…while Peter and his mother were the ones to suffer.

Peter had seen the anguish in his mother's eyes. The slump of her shoulders, the air of dejection she carried when her husband disappointed her yet again with late nights or canceled plans.

And Peter would be damned if he'd burden another woman with that type of lifestyle, the way his father had burdened his mother. Especially a woman he cared for.

Marriage, family, happily ever after…they weren't for him. His entire focus was on building his business and designing software to rival the competition. Which meant he had little or no time to devote to a relationship.

Even if he did…even if Reyware and Games of PRey were well-established enough to relax a bit, to go out and enjoy a healthy social life…he still wouldn't.

For Peter, it was all or nothing. He could concentrate all of his efforts on business, or he could concentrate all of his efforts on finding a wife and starting a family. He couldn't do both. And for now—probably for the next ten or twenty years—he chose to concentrate on his work.

It was a damn shame, though. Spending a few hours in the sack with Lucy might just have been worth losing time on a project or two.

The night of the charity event, Peter arranged for a limousine to pick Lucy up at seven o'clock. That gave her two and a half hours to get home from work, shower, change clothes, fix her hair and do her makeup.

It probably shouldn't have taken her half that long, but she wasn't used to attending high-priced dinners and fancy fund-raisers. And the thought of going with Peter, perhaps being mistaken for his latest bit of arm candy, had her stomach in knots.

Her apartment, only a few blocks from Peter's town house in downtown Georgetown, was small, but served its purposes. She'd bought several paintings from a local art gallery and framed some pictures of her family and friends to decorate the otherwise sparse white walls. Small area rugs added color to the brown pile carpeting, and the African safari images on her full-size bedspread made her room feel—in her opinion, anyway—wild and exotic.

And, of course, there was Cocoa, her beautiful, long-haired calico cat, who always rushed to the door to greet her, but ran from anyone else.

"Hello, baby," she cooed, heedless of the hairs covering her skirt and jacket as she swept the cat into her arms. Cocoa began to purr and nudge Lucy's chin with the top of her head.

"All right, all right. You're hungry, I know."

As was their habit, she set the feline on the kitchen table while she opened a can of Deluxe Dinner and chopped it up into bite-size pieces on a platter with pastel pawprints and Cocoa's name painted in flowing script.

"Enjoy your liver and chicken," she said with a kiss to the top of the cat's head. "I have a big party tonight and need to get ready."

Every item she intended to wear to the benefit lay strewn across her bed, for fear she might forget something. After a quick shower, she rubbed moisturizer into her steam-warmed skin and dabbed her pulse points with her favorite perfume. Then she blew her hair dry and began the painstaking process of getting dressed.

She started with the matching bra and panty set she'd bought to go with the red satin and black velvet gown before sliding on the black silk thigh-highs the saleslady had talked her into. Thigh-highs or stockings and a garter belt, the woman had assured her, were much sexier than panty hose.

Personally, Lucy questioned the need for sexy lingerie for a nondate with her boss. She could walk out to the limo naked and doubted he would spare her more than a glance before once again burying his nose in his laptop.

With the expensive gown molding to every curve of her body, she swept her hair up and fixed it into a loose French twist at the back of her head. Makeup and jewelry came next, and she pretended not to notice the slight tremor in her fingers as she applied mascara and lipstick.

This was ridiculous. She was a grown woman, attending a charity event to raise money for domestic violence victims and hopefully stir up interest in Peter's company. Not a geeky teenager attending the homecoming dance with the captain of the football team.

Steeling her spine with renewed determination, she slipped into high heels, grabbed the tiny sequined clutch with little more than a compact and lipstick inside and headed for the front door.

A glance at the microwave clock showed she was five minutes early, but if she headed downstairs now, she could meet the limousine when it arrived instead of making the driver buzz up for her.

She gave Cocoa one last stroke as the cat continued to lick her plate clean. "Be a good girl. I'll be home as soon as I can."

To her surprise, the limo pulled up just as she reached the double glass doors of her building. Draping a fringed black shawl around her shoulders, she went out to meet the car.

She half expected the driver to come around and hold

the door for her, but instead the door opened on its own. Her steps faltered as a foot emerged, followed by a leg, an arm and finally a head of sandy-blond hair. She'd thought Peter was simply sending a car for her, that she would meet him at the hotel where the dinner was being held. Now, it looked as though she would have to ride there with him. In the back of the limo. In close proximity.

He stood on the curb, waiting for her, looking like the California version of James Bond in his black tuxedo, and she had to remind herself to breathe, then put one foot in front of the other until she reached his side. He smiled brightly, letting his gaze slide over her as he reached out a hand for hers.

"If possible," he said, giving her fingers a gentle squeeze, "you look even more amazing tonight than you did yesterday."

The compliment washed over her like a warm breeze, causing the corners of her mouth to lift.

And then, from behind his back, he produced a single long-stemmed red rose. "For you. I thought you might appreciate it more than a corsage."

Although a small lump filled her throat at his thoughtfulness, she laughed. Peter could be incredibly charming when he wanted, but until this moment, she'd never been the recipient of that seductiveness.

She knew it wasn't real. He was only being polite for this one night because she was doing him a favor by accompanying him to the fund-raiser.

Still, for her, for now, it *was* real. And there was no reason she shouldn't enjoy it while it lasted. Soon enough—like first thing Monday morning—it would be back to work, back to their usual employer/employee relationship.

She lifted the bloom to her nose and inhaled its rich fragrance. "It's beautiful, thank you."

When their eyes met over the top of the rose, she thought she saw something deep and meaningful flash across his features, but it was just as quickly gone—if it had been there at all.

Clearing his throat, he moved away from the limousine and waved an arm for her to precede him. "Shall we?"

She nodded, stepping into the plush rear of the limo. Peter slid in beside her and the car rolled forward.

"Would you like something to drink?"

A bottle of champagne, already open, sat chilling in an ice bucket on the opposite seat. He poured a few inches of the golden liquid into a cut crystal glass and handed it to her before filling a flute for himself.

Lucy wasn't much of a drinker, and normally she never would have started in the car on the way to an event where she knew she would probably consume even more alcohol. But tonight, her nerves were jumping like kernels of corn over an open fire. Maybe a few sips of champagne would calm them down.

"Thank you again for coming with me," he said as the cool bubbles tickled their way down her throat. "I already feel more relaxed about the evening than if I were going alone or with a practical stranger."

If the majority of Peter's dates were "practical strangers," he certainly cozied up to them enough to invite them in at the end of the night.

She took another gulp of wine to wash away the depressing thought. Peter's love life was none of her business. His personal life was none of her business. Only his professional life, filling the hours from nine to five, were any of her concern. And sometimes a slice of overtime, such as tonight. But other than that, he could do whatever he wished with whomever he wished, and it wouldn't bother her a bit.

"This isn't a favor," she felt the need to clarify. "It's part of my job."

"Yes, but you didn't have to come along. You could have said you were busy, already had a date, or just plain refused."

She could have...if she'd thought of it.

The rest of the drive passed in silence until they pulled up in front of the Four Seasons on M Street, very close to the city limits of Georgetown. Peter set aside their empty glasses as the driver came around to open their door, then stepped out and turned back to offer Lucy his hand.

Arms linked, they walked into the elegant hotel lobby. A large banner and smaller, raised signs announced the City Women benefit and directed guests to the bank of elevators leading upstairs. Several couples were already there, and Peter and Lucy joined them.

The last ones in, they were at the front near the doors. She could feel the heat of Peter's hand at the small of her back, through the sheer material of her shawl. She tipped her head to look at him over her shoulder, noticing the thin line of his mouth, the tightness in his jaw. Her eyes narrowed, and she was about to ask if he was all right when the elevator doors opened with a swish. The pressure at her back increased as he urged her forward, into the plush, paneled hallway and in the direction of the crowded ballroom.

Round tables draped with hunter-green and pink linens to match the City Women's trademark colors filled the room, each seating ten to twelve people. At the front, a raised platform held long, rectangular tables on either side of a tall podium.

As soon as his eyes landed on the microphone he would be using for his acceptance speech, Peter made a choking sound and stuck a finger behind the collar of his shirt, as though the small black tie was cutting off his air supply.

"You'll be fine," she assured him, laying a hand on his elbow and running it down the length of his arm until their fingers twined. "Now we'd better get up there before Mrs. Harper-Whitfield starts 'yoo-hooing' for you over everyone's heads."

He groaned. "Please, no. Not Mrs. Harper-Whitfield."

Laughing, they started through the crowd, nodding and saying hello to acquaintances, stopping to chat only when they weren't given much choice. When they finally reached their seats, the City Women directors and founding members flocked to Peter's side, thanking him for coming, complimenting him on his latest donation or software creation.

Lucy sat beside him, a smile permanently etched on her face for the stream of admirers who paraded past, wanting a moment or two with the esteemed Peter Reynolds.

Finally dinner was served, and they were left mostly to themselves while everyone enjoyed delicious servings of thinly sliced beef, steamed broccoli, lightly seasoned new potatoes, and fruit tartlets for dessert. Hundreds of mingled voices filled the room, making a private conversation difficult.

Lucy realized, too, that Peter was inordinately nervous about getting up in front of such a large group. But no matter how slowly he ate, the meal was soon over and the City Women president was addressing the crowd, describing the organization's accomplishments of the past several months and relaying some very moving success stories.

As soon as the speaker began talking about that one special contributor who had helped to fill their shelters with computer equipment and offer women avenues other than remaining in abusive situations, Lucy felt Peter tense beside her. His entire body went taut, and his knuckles turned white where they tried to squeeze the life out of a poor, defenseless cloth napkin.

Turning unobtrusively in his direction, she leaned close enough to be heard and whispered, "Relax." She covered his clenched fist with the palm of her hand, gently stroking his warm skin until his grip on the linen loosened. Setting the napkin aside, she slipped her free hand beneath the lapel of his tuxedo jacket and retrieved the stack of index cards she knew would be there.

"Take a deep breath," she ordered in a soft, soothing tone. "You've done this a million times before, you'll be fine. And if all else fails, remember to picture everyone naked."

His head whipped around and his gaze, hot, green and intense, drifted over her, lingering a little too long on the area of her waist and breasts.

"Not *me*," she growled with a roll of her eyes, putting three fingers to his cheek and pushing him away.

The City Women president smiled brightly as she finished her introduction and the spotlight swung to Peter. Lucy shoved the note cards into his hand and urged him to his feet before joining in on the applause.

In the end, he had nothing to worry about. His speech was both funny and poignant, delivered with perfect pitch by a man who could flirt a nun out of her habit. Before he finished, Peter promised to continue refurbishing and donating used PCs for the organization's use, earning him a standing ovation and another round of boisterous applause. The City Women then gifted him with a plaque in appreciation of his aid.

From there, everyone moved across the hall to a second ballroom where an orchestra was set up to play for the rest of the night, as well as four cash bars that would split their profits with the hosting charity.

Now that his speech was over, Peter was much more relaxed and willing to mingle with a crowd that obviously adored him. And Lucy knew this was her cue to spring into action. To approach some of D.C.'s wealthiest citizens and talk up Peter's freshman software company, convincing them that any man who would volunteer so much time and money to such a worthy cause certainly deserved a modicum of support for his own interests. She would set up appointments for them to visit Peter at home, see samples of his work and discuss his plans for the future of Reyware.

Two long, exhausting hours later, Lucy had set up twenty-odd meetings for the following weeks and was fighting not to yawn and offend all the people she'd just spent half the night trying to impress.

Coming up behind her, Peter slid an arm around her waist, resting his chin on the slope of her shoulder. "Have we put in our time yet? Can we get the hell out of here?"

"I thought you were enjoying yourself," she said without turning around.

"Making the most of a bad situation…it's not quite the same thing. So how about it—wanna blow this Popsicle stand?"

She checked her watch. Nearly midnight. "I suppose it wouldn't be too terribly rude to leave now. We have been here for almost four hours."

"Feels like six. Besides, I want to get home and find a place to hang my new plaque." He waved the chunk of wood and gold plating in front of her as they made their way to the outskirts of the ballroom and sneaked off—*hopefully*—without being noticed.

The elevators were free, the doors sliding open as soon as Peter punched the down button. They were alone inside the carpeted, glass-walled car, and Lucy once again spotted signs of strain bracketing his mouth, his fingers clenching around the brass handhold that ran along all three sides.

"Do you have a problem with elevators?" she asked, drawing his attention from the glowing red numbers above the door.

"Elevators? No, why?"

"Because you seem awfully uncomfortable. I noticed it on the ride up earlier, too. We could have taken the stairs, you know."

He shook his head. "I'm fine. I just like getting off elevators more than I like getting on them."

That was an understatement, she thought, but didn't say anything more since they were only going from the fourth floor to the lobby. But then the lights flickered and Peter glanced up in alarm. A second later, the entire car went dark, lurching to a stop somewhere between floors as the cables and computerized panels groaned in protest.

"What's going on? Why aren't we moving?" Peter wanted to know, banging on the controls as though hitting all the buttons at once would miraculously send them back into motion.

"I think the power might be out," she told him, waiting for her vision to adjust to the pitch-black.

"Oh, God. How long do you think it will take them to get it back on?"

She shrugged and then realized he couldn't see her. "You know how these things are. Sometimes the electricity only flickers off for a few minutes, other times it takes all night."

"Oh, God," he groaned.

Peter's breathing echoed off the walls, heavy and exaggerated. She reached out, feeling for him, until her fingertips encountered the soft fabric of his tuxedo jacket.

"Take it easy, Peter. The elevator isn't even moving now."

"That's the problem," he gritted out, punctuating each word with a hard rap to the metal doors. "The damn thing isn't moving!"

A shiver of dread skated down her spine. "I thought you didn't like being in elevators because of that weird up-and-down sensation you get in your stomach."

"Ha!" The sound came out strangled and his breathing grew even more ragged. Beneath her hand, the muscles of his arm bunched and released.

"It's not *elevators,*" he snapped. "They haven't invented an elevator yet that moves fast enough for me. It's enclosed spaces. I can't stand small, enclosed spaces."

Three

Uh-oh.

"You're claustrophobic?"

How could he be claustrophobic? And how could she not know about it?

She'd been working with him for two years now. She knew his favorite foods, his favorite color, his favorite pair of boxer shorts, for heaven's sake. How could she have missed the fact that he was claustrophobic?

"Just a little."

His response came out on a wheeze and she realized he was seriously downplaying just how upset he was by this sudden set of circumstances.

"All right, let's not panic," she said, as much to herself as to him. She moved closer, rubbing his arm, his shoulder. "The power will probably come right back on. Until then, why don't you tell me how long you've had this little problem."

"Forever. Long as I can remember." A beat passed while he sucked in air like a drowning victim. "Is it hot in here? It's too hot in here."

She felt him struggling to shed his jacket even though she didn't think the temperature had gone up a single degree since the lights went off. His high level of anxiety probably had his internal thermostat going haywire.

"Here, let me help." She took the suitcoat, folding it in half and setting it aside in what she hoped was a safe corner.

"And what do you usually do when you find yourself in an enclosed space?" If she could keep him talking, maybe he wouldn't think so much about where they were. She might even get lucky and figure out a way to keep him calm until the elevator started moving again.

He laughed, a raw, harsh sound. "Go crazy? Throw up? Pass out?"

This was a side of Peter she'd never seen before. Sure, he was slightly scattered, a bit of a computer nerd. More focused on the new program he was designing than whether his hair was combed or there was enough milk in the refrigerator for breakfast.

But, other than the occasional round of public speaking, he was also strong and self-assured. So handsome, he made her teeth hurt. And he was in better physical shape than anyone would expect for a man who spent twenty-three hours of most days staring at a computer screen. He carried himself like a man with a mission; one who knew exactly why he'd been put on this earth and was simply going about the business of carrying out that task.

Little had she known he harbored this secret claustrophobia.

"Oh, God." He was punching buttons again, growing more agitated by the second. "We're going to die in here."

She bit down on her lip to keep from laughing out loud at that outrageous pronouncement. "We are *not* going to die. Come on. Come over here and sit down."

Taking his elbow, she tugged him away from the front of the elevator until they hit the rear wall. It took some doing, but she finally got him to the floor.

Covering his face with his hands, he muttered, "I don't feel very well. I think I might be sick."

"You're fine. Everything's going to be fine." She brushed his cheek with the back of her hand, finding it warm and damp with perspiration. "Close your eyes."

"What?"

"If your eyes are closed, you won't even know the lights are off. We'll talk and pretend we're back at the house, and before you know it, that's exactly where you'll be."

He gave a raspy chuckle. "I don't think that's going to work."

Running two fingers lightly over his eyelids, she whispered, "You never know until you try."

His chest still heaved with the speed of his breathing and she could feel his body shaking against her own.

"You're in your office," she murmured, thinking she sounded an awful lot like a hypnotist. "Working on the latest version of Soldiers of Misfortune, throwing in some extra severed heads and damsels in distress. The kids will love it."

"Too much violence. Should be more socially conscious."

She laughed at that, knowing how much time he spent worrying that his computer games were too mature for their audiences. "You're just socially conscious enough. Now focus. You're at your desk, swigging down your tenth can of soda…I'll be in any minute with your mail, and to chastise you for drinking too much of that sugar water."

"Nectar of the gods."

"The gods of Type-2 Diabetes, maybe." She played with the ends of his silky hair, trying to keep him from hurting himself as he banged his head rhythmically against the back wall of the elevator.

"You worry too much about me."

His comment caught her off guard, and for a minute she didn't respond. She did worry too much about him, but she couldn't help it. She cared about him, too—too much. She cared that he worked long hours and didn't get enough sleep, that he didn't eat right and inhaled cola like it was oxygen. And she cared that he was so upset about being stuck in this elevator in the middle of a blackout.

"Not too much," she said finally. "Just enough."

Was it her imagination, or was he calming down? His breathing didn't seem quite as loud now, and the fidgeting had slowed to a bare minimum.

A minute ticked by in silence while she waited to see if he was all right. If maybe he'd fallen asleep or really believed he was in his office, working on his latest Games of PRey installment.

But suddenly, the trembling started again, worse than before, and he shot to his feet. "This isn't working. We have to get out of here before we run out of air. Why isn't anyone trying to get us out?"

He pounded on the doors with his fists, shouting for help, on the verge of hyperventilating. Lucy made another grab for him, pulling him away, fighting the claustrophobia for his attention.

"Peter. Peter, stop. Listen to me." She framed his face with her hands, able to see the barest outline of his silhouette now that her eyes had adjusted to the darkness. "You're okay. Everything's going to be okay."

"No, no, no..." He shook his head emphatically, not listening or unwilling to believe. "I can't breathe."

She could feel the pulse at his throat beating out of control and knew she was losing him. But what else could she do? How did you calm someone who was on the brink of a breakdown?

The answer came to her in a flash and she didn't give herself time to second guess. Leaning up on tiptoe, she pressed her lips to his, kissing him as she'd always imagined. Her fingers slipped from his cheeks to his nape, tangling in the slightly long hair growing over his collar.

He tasted of scotch and heat and just plain Peter, and she wondered why she'd waited two years to do this. It was crazy, it was wrong, but it was also so darn good, her skin was threatening to melt right off her bones.

And best of all, Peter's panic seemed to have subsided. He wrapped his arms about her waist and dragged her closer, opening his mouth to let their tongues parry and thrust.

Their bodies rubbed together like two pieces of flint, all but shooting sparks. Her breasts, crushed to his chest, grew heavy and sensitive with desire, her nipples beading to nearly painful points. Lower, the hard line of his arousal nudged the area between her legs.

In the back of his mind, Peter knew he was supposed to be thinking about something. The dark, the broken-down elevator, getting out, or dying before anyone discovered them. But damned if he could find it in him to care about anything other than the warm, willing woman in his arms.

Lucy. He shouldn't be kissing Lucy…his assistant, his friend, the one person he didn't want to offend because, as he often joked, she knew where the bodies were buried.

But, God, she felt good. She smelled good, like flowers in springtime, with an overlaying scent of musk that made him think of hot, sweaty sex. And she tasted amazing.

Since puberty, he'd had his share of fantasies about making out with beauty queens and X-rated starlets; sometimes both at the same time. But no dream, no matter how erotic, could ever live up to what was happening right here, right now. She made steam rise from his pores and every drop of blood in his veins rush straight for the equator.

His hands slid from her waist to her buttocks, drawing her up and crushing her against the straining evidence of his enthusiasm. If they didn't stop soon, it would be too late.

But he had no intention of stopping. The ground would have to open up and swallow him whole. This elevator that had trapped them so securely would have to break from its cables and crush them like pancakes. Because unless an act of God pulled them apart, he was going to make love to Lucy Grainger.

Finally.

The lack of light heightened every sensation, the fireworks exploding behind his closed eyelids almost more than he could bear. He'd wanted her far too long to take things slow.

Letting his lips trail from her mouth to her chin, to

the tender flesh of her throat, he found the zipper at the back of her gown and slowly dragged it downward. His knuckles grazed her spine with each click of the zipper's teeth and she moaned, sending shivers of awareness through to his nerve endings.

As the barrier of her dress fell away, he unhooked the clasp of her strapless bra and cupped the two glorious globes of her breasts in the palms of his hands. His thumbs teased the nipples, drawing a gasp of pleasure from her parted lips.

Peter kissed her again, wanting to devour her, absorb her into his every pore. Her hands on his chest felt like iron brands. She fumbled with the buttons of his shirt until the tails came free of his pants. He reached up and yanked the bow tie from his neck before it choked him as she pushed the shirt off over his shoulders.

Her soft, delicate hands explored his body like a blind man exploring a work of art. Her sharp, manicured fingernails left trails of fire along his skin, making him want to growl low in his throat and take her like an animal. Only the knowledge that this was Lucy, a woman he cared about and would never intentionally hurt, kept him from throwing her down and driving into her right that second.

Instead he wrapped an arm around her back and lowered her slowly to the carpeted elevator floor. The shirt caught at his elbows hampered his movements, but he didn't want to waste time removing his cuff links and stripping down completely. Cradled in the hollow of her thighs, the gown bunched now around her hips, he let her thread her fingers into his hair and pull him down for a soul-stealing kiss.

Circling her ankle first, and then the sleek curve of her calf, he ran his hand over the satiny stocking encasing her leg. When he reached the top of her thigh, he found a wide band of elasticized lace and groaned. No panty hose to deal with, just sexy, convenient thigh-highs and a pair of barely there French-cut panties that could be slipped off in one quick motion or simply pushed aside when the time came.

Which would be soon. He couldn't last much longer, being this close to her, feeling her breasts with their pebbled peaks and the dampness of her desire soaking through her panties.

A muscle in his jaw jumped as his hand encountered that moisture and he rested his head against her brow for a moment, praying for the restraint it would take not to lose it then and there. But either God was on a break or Lucy was determined to shatter his self-control because she arched her back, ground her pelvis into his throbbing erection, and panted his name on a whisper of sound.

It was the name that did it. If she had only moaned or muttered nonsensical words, he might have kept it together. Hearing his name on her lips, though, realizing that she knew exactly who was touching her, making love to her, and that she had no intention of coming to her senses and asking him to stop, sent him straight over the edge.

Reaching between their hot, writhing bodies, he undid the front clasp of his slacks, shoving them down just enough to free his rigid length. At the same time, he stripped the flimsy satin triangle from her hips and spread her legs farther apart. With his hands on her bottom, he found the tight, feminine opening that beckoned him like a siren's song and entered her in one long, solid thrust.

Lucy cried out as Peter filled her. Her lungs felt ready to burst, her body burning with rising lust. She lifted her legs, crossing them at the ankles behind his back, and dug her nails into his shoulders, imploring him to move, to put an end to this torture.

"Please," she begged, surprised she could speak at all. Every fiber of her being vibrated with desire, pulsed with need. If he didn't bring her to orgasm soon, she thought, she just might die.

"Yes, please. Now."

His voice rasped like sandpaper as he pressed into her, then slowly began to retreat. In and out, his movements sending delicious shock waves through her system. The faster he thrust, the more rapid her breathing became. The tighter her insides wound. And when he slipped his fingers over the mound of curls, into her pulsating heat, to toy with the tiny nub of pleasure nestled there, she went wild.

Hips bucking, arms clutched around his back, her

inner muscles spasmed, milking him until he gave a low, guttural shout of completion and came inside her.

For long minutes after the most powerful climax of his life, Peter could do little more than lie there, sprawled across Lucy's supple body. Her heart pounded against his chest, keeping time with his own. Her nails clung to his back like talons, much as his dug into the cushiony flesh of her hips and buttocks. Her harsh breaths beat out a staccato rhythm in his ear and the pitch-black confines of the elevator car, echoing his own struggle to suck air into his deprived lungs.

And all he could think was that he'd just had earth-shattering, mind-blowing, rock-my-world sex with the one woman he'd sworn he would never touch.

The walls were beginning to close in on him again, but in a whole different way. Yes, the elevator felt stuffy and too small for his large frame. He wondered if they'd even have enough oxygen to survive until power was restored. But all of that drifted to the far reaches of his mind as he imagined the repercussions of what they'd just done.

He could lose her as his assistant, which would be more than a personal loss—it would be a blow to Rey-ware and the future of his program designs. She not only often gave him fresh ideas, but made it possible for him to work long hours without interruption.

He could lose her as a friend. He wasn't sure how to feel about that, since he didn't have many women friends and had never worried about forfeiting one of them before. He did know, though, that it would be tough not having her around. To talk to, to joke with, to ask for her opinion about everything from names for his latest games to which socks to wear with which shirt.

On the opposite side of the coin, he could be stuck with her. She might think this spontaneous bout of passion meant more than it did and expect him to feel the same way. She could want a relationship... commitment...marriage...

The very possibility sent fear stabbing through his bones like ice water. Wasn't that exactly what he'd been trying to avoid? He would be a terrible husband, an even worse father. He didn't think he had it in him at this point to be even a decent boyfriend or significant other.

If that's what it took to keep her from running, from leaving him for either another job or another man who could give her what she needed, then he would try. But he already knew he'd fail. It was in his genes.

He'd play the part of attentive lover...and relish every minute of the loving, he was sure. But soon enough, she would get tired of the hours he kept. Of being neglected when a new software program claimed more of his attention than she did. And that's when the resentment would begin, quickly turning into hate, and finally indifference.

Hadn't the exact same thing happened with his mother and father?

Lucy's sigh and the feel of her arms and legs falling from around his sweaty body brought him back to the present. He was probably crushing her. Lord knew he hadn't been as gentle as he could have been.

"I must be suffocating you. I'm sorry." As reluctant as he was to move, to draw away from her, he rolled to the side.

"It's all right," she said in a low voice. "I kind of liked it."

Her comment hit him like a punch to the gut. He wanted so much to be pleased by her words…but at the same time couldn't avoid worrying that it was simply the first step of an attitude that would soon become clinging.

Reaching out, he found her bare arm in the darkness and stroked from elbow to shoulder. "Did I hurt you?"

He heard a gentle tinkle and thought it must be her earrings as she shook her head.

"No," she answered aloud. "Did I hurt you?"

His bark of laughter bounced off the mirrored walls. That was Lucy for you; self-confident enough to believe she was just as capable of rough lovemaking as any man.

"Only in a good way, sweetheart."

As soon as the endearment passed his lips, he cringed. Bad move. What if she took it wrong? What if she thought he was inviting her to a whole new level of their relationship?

When she didn't respond, however, the moment of

alarm passed. Beside him, he heard her moving around and pushed to his feet.

"We should probably get dressed," he said, holding out his hand to help her up, and then leaning down to make contact when he realized she couldn't see the offer. "Never know when the power will come back on and the elevator doors will open."

"Wouldn't want that," she murmured.

Her removed tone reminded Peter that she was probably having second thoughts about their encounter, as well. Regrets.

That didn't sit well with him. As unsure as he was about what they'd done, about what the future might bring because of it, he didn't want Lucy to be sorry she'd let him make love to her. Hell, he wanted her eyes to still be glazed over, wanted to be the best lover she'd ever had.

But he couldn't have it both ways, could he? He had to either curl her toes and be ready for the possibility of building a relationship with her, or chalk it up to hot sex under duress and deal with the blow to his ego when she didn't fall at his feet, begging for more.

Patting their way around the floor of the car, they collected discarded pieces of clothing. It was impossible to identify them all, but they managed to zip up and rearrange their clothes just as the lights and buttons inside the elevator began to flicker.

Peter's stomach turned over in relief. He'd been okay, distracted as he was by this newest turn of events with Lucy. But if they'd been trapped much longer, he honestly couldn't be sure the claustrophobia wouldn't have come back and sent him hyperventilating again.

Eyes slowly adjusting to the return of fluorescent brightness, he stuffed an extra garment—likely his tie— in the pocket of his tuxedo jacket, watching Lucy tug at her gown, run a smoothing hand through her long black hair, and slide her toes back into a high-heeled shoe as the car gave a giant lurch and once again started its descent.

When the doors opened, he was relieved to find the lobby level fairly empty. A few people milled around, looking disoriented by the unexpected blackout, but in the process of going about their business.

As Peter and Lucy stepped out of the elevator, the hotel's manager raced up to them, offering effusive apologies for the inconvenience of being stuck between floors for so long. Peter waved off the man's worries. It wasn't the manager's fault he was claustrophobic, after all. And being trapped, even for such a short time, had given him the chance to finally make love to Lucy, which he couldn't bring himself to fully regret.

Instead Peter asked for the limo to be brought around. As they walked, he helped to arrange the shawl over Lucy's bare shoulders to protect her from the late-night chill.

Inside the limo, the air was warm and he instructed the driver to take them to her apartment first. The silence between them was stifling, growing more uncomfortable by the minute, and he racked his brain for something to say.

Thank you didn't seem quite appropriate. Nor did *I'm sorry.*

He wanted to ask her to come home with him, to stay the night and let him touch her again the way she had in the elevator. Only this time, he would go more slowly...explore those luscious curves in more detail, study every nook and cranny of her beautiful body.

Stealing a glance at her still form out of the corner of his eye, he felt himself grow hard with wanting her again.

So much for scratching an itch or thinking would ever be enough when it came to Lucy Grainger.

The car pulled to a stop outside her building, and Peter escorted her to her apartment. She didn't speak as they climbed the stairs, and he couldn't think of any way to fill the awkward quiet.

At her door, he touched her arm, tried to take her hand, but she pulled away. "Lucy..." he began.

"Good night, Peter," she said, cutting him off and making it clear she wasn't interested in conversation. "I'll see you on Monday."

And then she turned the key in the lock and disappeared inside.

With a heavy sigh, he slid his hands into the pockets of his jacket and let his forehead fall against the cool grain of her mahogany paneled door. His brows drew together as his fingers burrowed into a strange silkiness.

Pulling his hand back out of the pocket, he found himself staring down at Lucy's lacy black panties. A shudder rocked his tall frame and for a moment he thought his knees might buckle.

If her panties were out here, with him, that meant she had been naked underneath her gown on the ride home. God, he was glad he hadn't known that then or he'd have been hard-pressed not to jump her a second time.

He remembered being inside her. The hot, wet haven of her body, clasping and clenching, driving him insane.

Hot. Wet. Skin to skin.

His eyes fell shut as realization and dread washed over him. He hadn't worn a condom. He wasn't sure he'd had a condom with him to wear, even if the thought *had* occurred to him back in that elevator. Before she'd spun every sane notion from his head with her kisses.

He hadn't worn a condom and didn't know whether or not she was on birth control. Which meant she could be pregnant. With his child.

Oh, this night just kept getting better and better.

Four

When Lucy arrived at work Monday morning, she stood on Peter's front stoop for several long minutes, key in the lock and hand on the knob, trying to convince herself it would be business as usual once she stepped inside.

And why wouldn't it? What happened Friday night in the elevator meant nothing, right? It had been a fluke. An intimate encounter brought on by crisis conditions, and not something that would have ever come about under normal circumstances.

But that didn't explain why Peter had called so many times over the weekend. Thank God she'd let the machine pick up the first time…and every time after that.

With the volume down, she'd almost been able to survive those four rings each time without her heart jumping straight out of her chest.

And then he'd shown up at her door Sunday afternoon. She'd stared through the peephole, bouncing anxiously on the balls of her feet, breathing hard, and biting the inside of her lip to keep from making a sound. He'd looked rumpled and ruffled, and more aggravated the longer he stood outside her apartment, waiting for her to answer.

She felt like a coward, afraid to face her own boss. Which was the only reason she'd come to work today instead of calling in sick. If she didn't, she was afraid she'd never be able to face Peter again.

Taking a deep, fortifying breath, she turned the knob and stepped inside, closing the door silently behind her. On tiptoe, she made her way into the den that housed her work area, quickly but quietly putting away her purse and shrugging out of her linen suit jacket.

With any luck, she wouldn't see Peter for another few hours. Hopefully he'd had another long night and would sleep until noon. And maybe by then she could come up with an excuse to leave early or run some errands outside of the office.

How long do you think you can keep that up? a voice in her head whispered. Sneaking around, avoiding him as much as possible.

If she knew Peter…and after two years, she felt she did…he wouldn't put up with that sort of thing for long. Unless—if she was lucky—he wanted to avoid her, too. Unfortunately, fifteen phone calls and an impromptu trip to her apartment told her that probably wasn't the case.

"Lucy?"

Peter's voice, raised and eager, floated down to her from the second floor. Then she heard his weighted footsteps as he jogged down the carpeted stairs and let her head fall forward over her computer's keyboard. Oh, boy, here it came. The confrontation.

She straightened in her chair a moment before Peter appeared in the doorway, looking even more scattered and unkempt than yesterday when he'd shown up on her doorstep.

He was in his stocking feet and wore a pair of faded jeans that rode low on his narrow hips. The denim was wrinkled, as was the cotton of his plain white T-shirt, making her wonder if he'd slept in his clothes—and for how long.

"Lucy." Her name came out part huff, part sigh. He ran both hands through his hair, leaving sandy-blond spikes sticking up here and there.

"I've been waiting for you all day," he said, apparently unaware that it was only nine in the morning. "I called your apartment a dozen times over the weekend. I even ran over to see you on Sunday. Where the hell have you been?"

She opened her mouth to tell him it was none of his business, but he shook his head, waving a hand in the air to cut her off.

"Never mind, it doesn't matter. We have to talk."

Her stomach fell to her knees as he dragged a chair over and sidled up to her desk, getting right to the point.

"Lucy," he began, elbows balanced on his thighs, hands clasped between his spread legs.

But she couldn't stand to hear him talk about what a lapse in judgment that night in the elevator had been, how they were employer and employee, and he didn't feel that way about her.

"Peter," she cut him off, not quite meeting his gaze. "I know what you're going to say, and I agree one hundred percent. What happened the other night was a mistake. We were caught off guard by the blackout and being unexpectedly trapped in that elevator. Neither of us would have indulged in such behavior otherwise, and I'm sure we never will again. Let's just forget it and go back to business as usual."

Peter sat back, intently studying Lucy's face. The alabaster skin, the sparkling violet shadow shading her black-lined eyes, the red-hot lipstick glossing her full, kissable mouth. She had a small beauty mark to the left and a little above the corner of that mouth, making him want to lean in and swipe his tongue across it for a quick taste.

Speak for yourself, he thought. She might believe their sexual encounter after the charity dinner was brought on solely by the lack of electricity and his unfortunate bout of claustrophobia, but what she didn't realize was that he'd been fantasizing about making love to her for a very long time.

Sure, the city-wide blackout had spurred him into taking actions he probably would have otherwise managed to control, but he wouldn't go so far as to say it never would have happened. And he most certainly wasn't going to forget it anytime soon.

As if that was even possible.

Still, it was a relief to hear she was prepared to brush the incident under the rug rather than turning it into something it wasn't or expecting more from him than he was willing or ready to give. That made one element of the situation easier, but not the portion he'd spent the weekend working up the courage to discuss with her.

"That may be easier said than done." He kept his tone low and serious enough to catch her undivided attention. Finally she raised her head and met his gaze directly.

"What do you mean?"

Instead of blurting out his primary concern, he tried to broach the subject in a more delicate way. "I don't suppose you're on the Pill," he said, and then realized that was about as subtle as a bull in a china shop.

Immediately her hackles went up. She stiffened, leaning away from him and folding her arms beneath her breasts. Those luscious, mouthwatering breasts that he'd kissed and fondled only two days ago. It was enough to bring his body to full, highly aroused attention and force him to shift in his seat for a more comfortable position.

Brow furrowed, Lucy crossed her legs, driving her

skirt up a good two inches and jiggling a high-heeled foot—which didn't help one bit—before snapping, "What business is that of yours?"

"None," he said carefully, "until Friday night. We didn't, um, use any form of protection. Unless…"

He let the word hang, watching realization dawn in her sapphire eyes. Hoping against hope that she'd laugh and slap him on the back and tell him not to worry, she'd been taking birth control for years. Instead, the color washed from her face while at the same time two rosy flags of embarrassment bloomed on her cheeks.

Something cold and ominous settled low in his belly. "I take it that's a no."

The muscles in her throat convulsed as she swallowed. "No," she croaked, giving an almost zombielike shake of her head. "There was no reason to be taking anything. And I always thought that if the situation presented itself, we'd both be smart enough to use a condom."

A wry smile curved his lips. "Yeah, me, too. Guess we both went brain dead there for a while."

Taking a deep breath, he got to his feet and began to pace. "As careless as we were, what's done is done. Now we just have to figure out what to do about it."

Silence filled the room for several long minutes, the only sound the tick-tock of the grandfather clock drifting in from the foyer. And then Lucy seemed to collect herself. She uncrossed her legs, unfolded her arms and stood.

"This is ridiculous, Peter. We're jumping to conclusions, fretting over nothing. What are the chances of my becoming pregnant from that one short encounter?"

"Spoken like any number of single mothers just before the stick turned blue."

She shot him a quelling glance. "All I'm saying is that we shouldn't borrow trouble. I'm sure there's nothing to worry about."

"I hope you're right," he said slowly, "but all the same, when will we know?"

A blank expression washed over her features, and then it donned on her what he was asking. Once again, her cheeks blushed pink.

"I'm not, um…a few weeks, I guess."

Weeks. Great. Peter made a mental note to stock up on antacid. Waiting days, let alone weeks, to find out if she was pregnant with his child was bound to give him the mother of all ulcers.

He wanted to demand an answer now. Drag her to the nearest drugstore for one of those over-the-counter tests and insist she take it. Of course, it probably wouldn't tell them much. He knew next to nothing about women's cycles and symptoms of pregnancy, but thought it took more than a few days to be able to tell about these types of things.

So he would be patient—swig his antacid, watch her like a hawk and wait until they knew for sure.

Lucy stepped out of the downstairs powder room tucked beneath the stairwell and nearly jumped to find

Peter staring at her from the other side of the kitchen island. She rolled her eyes, tamped down on the annoyance that seemed to be brimming too close to the surface these days and headed back to her office.

What did he want from her? she wondered, not for the first time. It had been three days since he'd brought up the topic of an unexpected pregnancy. And since then, he'd followed her around like a shadow. He was always nearby, asking if she needed anything, watching her every movement. It was as though he expected her to sprout feathers or in some other way show outward signs of carrying his child.

If only it were that easy. Truth be told, the waiting was driving her crazy, too.

She'd bought a pregnancy test on her way home from work Monday, after spending the day on eggshells, pretending his pronouncement that they hadn't used protection didn't concern her a bit. The test had come up negative, but that only served to increase her sense of anxiety.

Maybe the test was wrong. Maybe it was too early for an over-the-counter method to show accurate results. Maybe one of these days—since she'd bought out the corner store's supply and taken to running one each morning before she left the apartment—the stick would show a plus sign instead of a minus one and her whole world would come crashing down around her ears.

That thought sent a lead weight of dread straight to the bottom of her stomach.

She should call her doctor and make an appointment so she could get a definitive answer once and for all. But, God help her, she couldn't bring herself to do that. She was too frightened of what he might tell her.

What if she was pregnant?

Her initial response had been elation. Pregnant. With Peter's baby. Wasn't that the twist her overactive imagination often took when she pictured the two of them together? There were dating scenarios, seduction scenarios, marriage scenarios, family scenarios, even retirement scenarios for when their children were grown and they were once again alone in the house as the ripe old age of sixty.

Under the right circumstances, she would be delighted to be having a baby with Peter. The way things stood between them now, however, she couldn't think of a worse development.

If it turned out she was pregnant, Peter would likely offer to marry her, or at least insist on being involved in the child's life. That's the kind of man he was.

But he would resent Lucy for locking him into a situation he wanted no part of. The child would be a constant reminder of the mistake he'd let himself make one night in an elevator in the middle of a blackout, and of the freedom he'd lost because of it.

She didn't want that. It would be better, she thought, to leave. Go somewhere else, raise the child on her own, and never let Peter know he'd been right about their lack of birth control producing a child.

Not that she could ever bring herself to do such a

thing. A child deserved to know its father...and a father deserved to know about his child. Besides, Peter could be like a dog with a bone. He wouldn't rest until he knew for sure, and if she went away, no doubt he would track her down. With his computer skills and contacts all over the world, he would find her, if only to get a final answer to his question.

But she was getting ahead of herself. The smart thing would be to find out whether or not she actually was pregnant before making any drastic plans on how to handle the situation.

Without so much as a creak of the hardwood floor in warning, Peter appeared in the archway of the den, once again startling her out of her reverie. Lucy put a hand to her heart in an effort to slow its erratic pace. If he didn't stop sneaking up on her, she was going to tie a bell around his neck.

"Is everything okay?" he asked.

He was wearing a pair of dove-gray dress slacks today, with a casual, light blue button-down shirt. His feet were bare, as was his habit, and which probably accounted for his ability to move silently through the house. Leaning a shoulder against the carved wood molding of the doorjamb, his green eyes ran over her intently, making her squirm.

Turning back to her computer screen, she did her best to act impervious. "Fine."

"Is there anything I can get you?" he pressed. "Juice, water, a sandwich?"

She'd eaten lunch less than an hour ago, and she noticed he didn't offer to bring her coffee or tea, which might be harmful to a growing fetus. Little did he know she helped herself to a cup or two each morning before leaving her apartment. Of course, she'd switched to naturally decaffeinated, just in case. She honestly didn't believe there was any reason to be concerned, but on the off chance she *was* pregnant, she wasn't willing to risk eating or drinking anything that might hurt her— possibly imaginary—unborn child.

"No, thank you," she answered. And then a beat passed and she changed her mind. "On second thought, I could use a glass of milk. My stomach has been a little upset lately, so maybe that would help."

Peter blanched, the muscles in his face going slack as he pushed himself away from the wall and stood there for a fraction of a second before nodding stiffly and darting toward the kitchen.

She shouldn't have done it. It was cruel to play on Peter's fears about an unplanned pregnancy. But his hovering and endless stream of inquiries about her health and daily well-being were beginning to grate on her nerves.

When he returned with her glass of milk, she would apologize and tell him she was fine—no outward hints of impending motherhood so far. But for now, she leaned back in her chair, let her head fall over the hard cherry wood edging, and laughed until every drop of stress and strain that had built up over the past few days drained out of her body and left her feeling much, much better.

"So, are you coming to the club tonight for a drink?"

Peter shook his head, his breathing labored as he fought to raise the hundred pound barbell over his head.

"Thirty-nine. Forty." Ethan Banks, his best friend and spotter counted off for him. They tried to meet at the gym at least three times a week for a full workout and to catch up on current events…or in Ethan's case, current conquests.

Ethan owned The Hot Spot, a local Georgetown nightclub that drew in a bevy of handsome men and lovely young ladies looking to party. It was the ladies Ethan liked the most, and according to him, he took a different one home with him every night. With his dark good looks and sparkling smile, Peter supposed it could be true.

"Forty-six. Wanna get together Sunday for the baseball game?"

Peter shook his head again. "Huh-uh."

"How about letting me bring a couple girls over later and we'll get a group thing going? Forty-nine. Fifty."

"No." His brows drew together as he sat up and wiped the sweat from his face and neck with a towel. "Wait a minute. What did you say?"

Ethan chuckled. "I thought that might get your attention. You've been distracted all night. Care to tell me what's going on?"

With a sigh, Peter got up and moved to the bank of treadmills along the far wall. Ethan followed, stepping onto the machine next to him and adjusting his speed.

For long minutes, Peter said nothing. His relationship with Lucy was nobody's business and he didn't particularly relish the idea of telling his best friend he was waiting to find out if the rabbit died, so to speak.

But it was clawing at him. Every moment of his time with Lucy in that elevator. Every day since, wondering how that night would change things between them and whether he was about to become a father.

Maybe talking it over with his friend would help. Ethan might be a ladies' man, but he had a good head on his shoulders. If he ribbed Peter too much about his indiscretion with his assistant, though, Ethan would find his teeth at the back of his throat.

"You know Lucy, right?" he said finally, after they'd both jogged at a leisurely pace for about half a mile.

"Of course," Ethan replied with a wicked grin. "I've only been trying to get her to come work for me and eventually come to bed with me since the day you hired her. Has she changed her mind? Is that what you're trying to tell me?"

"Hell, no." Annoyed, Peter snapped his head around to glare at his friend's cocky expression and nearly lost his footing. Regaining his balance, he said, "Lucy isn't interested in you. Let it go."

"Never say die, man. They all fall for my potent charms eventually."

"You wish," Peter answered with a snort. "Look, you wanted to know what was going on, so just shut up and listen, okay?"

"Okay, okay, I'm listening. Spill. What's up with Lucy?"

"You remember the big blackout that hit last Friday night?"

Ethan swore. "How could I forget? The club was a madhouse, trying to find flashlights and keep everyone from panicking and causing a stampede."

"Yeah, well, it wasn't a shining moment for me, either."

"Why, what happened?"

"I attended that City Women benefit with Lucy."

"The one where they were giving you the award? Cool. How'd it go?"

"I'm getting to that." Peter reached out to click the speed dial up another notch, making it harder to talk, but burning off some of the excess energy that had been crawling under his skin since he'd made love to Lucy. "Lucy and I sneaked out around midnight. We were in the elevator, on the way down to the lobby, when the power cut off."

"Oh, man. I'll bet you had fun. Did it get bad?"

Ethan had known about his claustrophobia for years, and since he wasn't speaking loudly enough for anyone else in the room to hear, Peter didn't feel embarrassed at having it brought up.

"It wasn't fun," he admitted. "But that wasn't the worst part."

"There's a worst part?"

Peter shot him another aggravated glance at his continued interruptions. This was difficult enough to get out, both because of the topic and the workout he was getting.

"I slept with her," he blurted.

"What?" Ethan stumbled, grabbing onto the treadmill's sidebars and saving himself at the last minute. "Whoa," he muttered in a low voice. "Are you serious?"

Peter's mouth twisted. "As a snake bite."

"So…was she good?"

The look Peter pierced his friend with this time was hot enough to burn. "None of your damn business. And don't talk about her that way."

Ethan threw his arms up in surrender. "Hey, take it easy. We always share the four-one-one about women and how they were in the sack."

"Yeah, well, this is different. It's Lucy. Don't talk about her that way," he said again.

Peter knew he was acting strangely. He didn't want his friend thinking there was more going on between him and his assistant than a regrettable one-night stand, but defending her honor that way had definitely clued him in. He should have kept his mouth shut or simply shrugged and said she was great. Then maybe Ethan wouldn't be eyeing him like he was afraid Peter's skin was about to peel back to reveal some alien life form.

"Fine. Sorry. So you two did the dirty deed. Is there a problem? Is she getting all clingy and romantic?"

Ha! If this past week was Lucy's idea of clingy and romantic, he'd hate to see her give him the brush-off.

"No, it's not that," he said instead. "We, um…didn't use a condom, and now there's a chance she might be pregnant."

Ethan didn't trip over his own feet at that pronouncement, but he did let loose a string of curses blue enough to turn the heads of other gym patrons. Peter cringed and waited to hear what his friend of ten years would say about his responsibilities and failure to practice safe sex.

"Damn. She's not stringing you along, is she? Buy one of those tester things or take her to the doctor and find out for sure, but don't let her sucker you into anything."

For a moment, Peter let his anger at Ethan's low estimation of Lucy's character simmer through his veins. And then he realized it wasn't really Lucy his friend thought so little of, it was all women.

Ethan met too many frivolous, promiscuous women at his club and was dumb enough to go home with them. He'd probably never met a tasteful, genuine woman like Lucy. To Ethan, women were gold diggers, or party girls, or steel-heeled bitches who would as soon emasculate a man as look at him. So, of course, his first thought would be that Lucy was using a pregnancy angle to trap Peter.

Thankfully, Peter didn't believe it for a minute.

"It's not that. Lucy wouldn't do something like that.

And before you ask—" he lifted a hand to stop his friend's tirade before it began "—I know because it isn't Lucy's style. My problem is a hell of a lot bigger than 'is she or isn't she?' or what her motives might be."

Ethan wiped sweat from his forehead with the back of his arm, his mouth turned down in a frown at Peter's refusal to consider ulterior motives. "Oh, yeah? What's that?"

Peter swallowed, trying to put the thoughts that had been swirling around in his brain for the past week into words. "The problem," he said, "is that I'm kind of hoping she is."

Five

Two Mondays later, Lucy knew what her future held…and it wasn't Peter or a baby. The knowledge hurt more than she'd anticipated, sending a low throb of disappointment through her entire system.

Shaking off the light sprinkling of rain from the short walk to Peter's brick-fronted row house, she stepped inside and braced herself for his immediate appearance. Surprisingly he didn't materialize at the top of the stairs to greet her, but she heard the sounds of movement coming from the kitchen.

After hanging her raincoat in the hall closet and stowing her purse in the bottom drawer of her desk, she headed for the back of the house. Peter stood at the counter, scooping coffee grounds into a filter.

She leaned forward against the island, her fingers clutching the edge of the cool marble. Taking a deep breath, she said, "I'll take a cup of that when it's ready."

He fixed her with a laser-sharp gaze as he finished what he was doing and punched the button to start the coffee brewing. "Are you sure that's a good idea?"

She nodded. It was an odd way to break the news to him, but easier than anything else she'd come up with.

"It's fine. I got my period this morning," she admitted with more than a little embarrassment.

A minute ticked by while he stared in stony silence. It wasn't quite the reaction she'd expected. A sigh of relief or maybe a few handsprings. Instead he seemed almost…reticent.

"I don't know what to say," he finally replied. "'I'm sorry' doesn't seem quite appropriate, but then neither does 'I'm glad.'"

"Are you?" she asked softly. "Glad or sorry?"

He stepped forward, rolling his shoulders as he stuffed his hands into the front pockets of his jeans. "I honestly don't know, Luce. A part of me feels like we dodged a bullet. But another part of me… You know, it might have been nice to be a father."

Lucy felt the same way, but was dismayed to hear Peter say as much. And then her eyes began to mist, surprising her even more. She blinked quickly and cleared her throat, moving to the refrigerator to hide her sudden rush of emotion.

What was wrong with her? For the past two weeks, she'd been worried she might be pregnant from a spontaneous intimate encounter with her boss…a man she'd been attracted to for years, but who had never shown a trace of attraction himself before the night of the charity dinner. And now she was getting weepy because she *wasn't* carrying his child? If that was the case, she seriously needed her head examined.

Grabbing the orange juice jug from the top shelf, she stalked across the kitchen and retrieved a glass from the cupboard, careful to give Peter a wide berth. She poured a few inches of juice and swallowed it.

"At least things can go back to normal now," she said when she thought her voice was steady enough not to shake.

"Yeah." His reply was low and dispassionate. He turned, starting out of the kitchen without the coffee he'd spent so much time preparing. "I'll be upstairs, working."

She watched him go, wondering about his strange behavior. When had he started thinking about family and fatherhood? And had he really been considering having them with her?

It didn't make sense. Peter had never shown the least bit of interest in her before, and she knew for a fact that what had happened in the elevator was merely a result of his claustrophobia. If he hadn't been desperate for an escape from his panic and she hadn't been so readily available, there was no doubt in her mind that matters between them would have continued in the usual pattern. She would have shown up on time for work each morning, trying to ignore the sweet ache of longing that coursed through her every time she looked at Peter, and he would have continued to treat her as nothing more than a valued and competent employee.

Instead he'd caught her at a weak moment, when she'd let her longtime attraction to him merge with her concern over his reaction to the blackout, until she'd convinced herself that he wanted to make love to her as much as she did to him.

A person was entitled to make one mistake in her life, wasn't she? One huge, throbbing, monumental mistake.

The coffeemaker on the counter sputtered and Lucy poured herself a cup, doctoring the dark, fragrant brew with a sprinkle of sugar and dollop of milk.

The funny part was that, despite everything, Lucy thought they probably would have been able to put the weekend's incident behind them and return to their normal routine…if it hadn't been for that little pregnancy scare.

And that's what confused her the most. Peter should be relieved; dropping to his knees, thanking God their one indiscretion hadn't put an end to his carefree bachelor lifestyle. But when she'd told him she wasn't pregnant, he'd acted almost…disappointed.

Could that be right? Could he have *wanted* a baby?

No. She shook her head, carrying the steaming mug back to her office in the den. It was silly to think Peter might have wanted a child. Especially now, especially with her.

If he was beginning to consider settling down, then he would want to find a nice woman to marry and have children with. He wouldn't be hoping a one-night stand with his assistant—a woman he'd never looked at twice before—would result in surprise fatherhood.

She must be reading the situation wrong. For all she knew, he was upstairs right now, dancing a jig and e-mailing his buddies to tell them about his near brush with disaster.

Which is exactly what she should be doing. She didn't want to be a single mother any more than she wanted to be the wife of a man who'd only married her because they forgot to use a condom.

Taking a sip of the still-warm coffee, she pulled her chair closer to the desk and doggedly decided to put this entire fiasco with Peter and their nonexistent baby behind her and get down to business.

But that didn't keep her heart from squeezing or her eyes from growing damp at the thought of what might have been.

Peter sat in front of his blank computer monitor, struggling to wrap his mind around what he was feeling.

Lucy wasn't pregnant. There was no baby. And damned if he didn't think he might be sorry about it.

He probably shouldn't have projected so far into the future, but he'd let himself imagine, let himself plan…Lucy, pregnant from their single encounter the night of the city-wide power outage. Taking responsibility for his actions and asking her to marry him. Watching her grow round as a pumpkin with his baby inside her.

He'd pictured her in his house, living here, belonging here. Making love to her every night. Holding her in his arms in a tangle of sheets while they slept and then waking the same way every morning.

For a man who'd sworn he would never tie himself down with a wife and family, those images had gotten pretty damn specific.

And while he wouldn't mind having Lucy in his bed—just once or twice more to get his fill—he supposed he should be glad things were working out this way.

Having a child at this point in his life just wasn't feasible. He wasn't a man to neglect his responsibilities, and if he'd married Lucy and had a child with her, he would have felt the need to spend time with them. Lord knew he'd want to be a better father to his children than his father had been to him.

And a better husband. He might not have planned it, but he genuinely liked Lucy, and if they'd made a baby together, then he would have done his best to treat her right, too. Which meant he could kiss Reyware and Games of PRey goodbye.

A wave of dread washed over him, followed by the cool, cleansing breeze of relief. Yes, it was definitely better this way.

If Lucy had wound up pregnant, he'd have married her and turned his focus on her and their child…maybe even someday children. But his own lousy childhood had taught him that he couldn't have a family and run a successful business, so he would have had to give up his thriving software company and look for some other, less demanding job. Probably computer repair, which was about all he thought he'd be good at.

He shuddered at the thought. He'd have changed diapers and played horsey and done everything in his power to let his children know he loved them, but he would have been miserable working nine to five for someone else just to keep food on the table.

Maybe someday, after he'd made a few billion dollars and could afford to hire a staff of corporate go-getters to run things for him, then maybe he'd start thinking about finding a woman to settle down with and having a couple kids. If Lucy was still available at that point, he might even consider hooking up with her again.

But for now…For now, this was good. Hell, it was freaking fantastic. He'd really lucked out. Slipped the noose, so to speak.

And it probably wouldn't take long at all for Lucy

and him to get back to their old camaraderie, their old habit of working together like a well-oiled machine. She already looked more recovered from their encounter than he felt, thank goodness. He'd have hated to have her hanging on him, expecting their relationship to change, take on new meaning.

If it took him a while to get the memory of her warm, writhing body out of his head, well, that was nobody's problem but his own. No one needed to know he still felt her beneath him at night while he struggled to fall asleep. Or that just the sight and smell of her sent a shock of awareness through his bloodstream.

Those things would haunt him, *Lucy* would haunt him the rest of the time they worked together. Maybe even forever.

Days turned into weeks as Peter and Lucy functioned around each other like virtual strangers. She came to work every day on time, went through the motions, took care of him as well as she ever had. Anyone looking in at them would think they had the perfect employer/employee relationship.

Only Peter—and Lucy, if she were being honest—knew that was far from the truth. The air between them fairly sizzled with tension and sexual electricity. He expected sparks to shoot from his fingertips every time she sauntered into his office and handed him the morning mail or a fresh cup of coffee, and he couldn't remember the last time he'd had a decent night's sleep.

Lucy might look like a model stepping straight off the runway, more beautiful every time he looked at her, but he was beginning to feel like something the dog dragged in. Exhaustion and hot, ceaseless desire were taking their toll.

He leaned back in his desk chair, rubbing his eyes and running a hand through his hair. The letters, numbers and symbols making up the codes on his computer screen jumbled together as his vision blurred.

Even his work was suffering, he thought with frustration, though he tried hard to not let it show. And Lucy, bless her, was a pro at fielding questions and making excuses for how busy he was.

But William Dawson, a client in New York, was a different story. He'd been badgering Peter to fly up, look over his company's computer system and design a plan to upgrade and get things running more smoothly and cost-effectively. It was a reasonable request, one he'd honored numerous times in the past.

Peter had worked with Dawson before and knew him to be a good guy who would pay Peter's hefty fee on time and use his powerful influence and word-of-mouth to send more business Peter's way.

Darned if he could work up the least bit of enthusiasm about it, though. Getting far away from Lucy would probably be the smart thing to do. Give them both some breathing room, hopefully help to dispel the taut, sensual awareness buzzing around them like a hive of horny little honeybees.

But something in his gut, in the back of his brain warned against it. A niggling sense that if he left town, Lucy might not be here when he got back.

She'd been acting strangely since that night at the Four Seasons. Keeping to herself as much as possible, avoiding his gaze when she couldn't.

Not that he blamed her, but she was a talented, educated woman who could get a job with anyone, doing almost any kind of work in the city. And he was afraid if he went somewhere, left her alone for even a short amount of time, she would decide things between them had grown too strained and would begin looking for a position elsewhere.

He didn't want that, and if he had any say at all, he wouldn't allow it. Which meant he couldn't take off for Manhattan without knowing what Lucy planned to do while he was gone.

Unless...

He blinked and sat up straighter in his chair, halting the swivel motion.

The trip to New York would be business-related, and Lucy was his assistant. He could ask her to go along. No, insist. They could fly up, stay a couple of nights in a nice hotel, then fly home. That way, he'd know where Lucy was at all times and she wouldn't get the chance to do something stupid like leave him.

Now he just had to figure out how to convince Lucy that her presence was required on a job he'd always before accomplished on his own. He sat there, spinning back and forth in slow circles, biting his way through a small stack of pencils while his mind raced.

She was going to balk. She probably would have even before they'd slept together, but now that they had, she'd be less inclined to travel with him in such close confines and possibly share a hotel suite or connected rooms.

At the thought of spending so much time with her, his blood thickened and things began to stir below the equator. Lucy, however, would probably have the exact opposite response. At least, she'd shown no signs so far of being attracted to him or wanting to repeat that night's performance.

He didn't know whether to take that as an insult against his sexual prowess or simply her way of distancing herself from what she considered a lapse in professionalism.

Well, this was getting him nowhere. Slapping his hands on his knees, he stood and headed for the hall. He heard the almost musical tap of Lucy's keyboard drifting upstairs from her office and started down the steps, one hand on the smooth mahogany banister.

Though she didn't stop what she was doing or acknowledge him in any way, he knew she sensed his proximity the minute he crossed the threshold into the den by the slight pause in her frantic typing. She recovered quickly and kept working, eyes on the screen, pretending he wasn't there—which she'd gotten pretty good at over the past few weeks. Her disinterest annoyed him, but he swallowed back the urge to confront her, to make her notice him on a personal, primitive level, and walked forward.

Lucy did her best to ignore Peter as he waltzed into her office and made himself at home by propping a hip on the edge of her desk. The faded plaid boxer shorts he'd been wearing for two days now left his legs bare and put a hairy, well-muscled thigh nearly at eye level and definitely too close for comfort.

He was beginning to look tired and run-down. Not for the first time, she thought about telling him to take a shower and climb into bed for a much-needed nap, just as she had a thousand times before. But that brought to mind images of Peter naked…wet and soapy, on a soft, wide mattress, on top of her, inside of her… It was enough to drive a person mad, so she bit down on her lip and said nothing.

"Are you ever going to look at me?"

"Not if I can help it," she tossed back. And then she did, because there really wasn't any other choice. "What do you want, Peter? I'm very busy, trying to keep your business afloat."

"And I appreciate it," he said cockily, "but this is business-related, too."

That got her attention. Reluctantly she lifted her hands from the keyboard and sat back, meeting his green and hazel gaze for the first time since he'd entered the room.

"All right, I'm listening."

"So you're a protective pet owner," he teased with a grin. "I don't blame you. How would you feel about a male pet sitter, though? Would that be okay?"

She studied him carefully, wondering what he was getting at to show such interest in Cocoa's well-being. "Of course. Why?"

"I know a guy…" he told her cryptically, shrugging one shoulder. "If you can't find anyone else you'd be satisfied with, let me know and I'll see if he's available."

"All right." She wasn't sure what to think of Peter's helpfulness, but it seemed he was willing to call in a few favors with his friends just to get her to go to New York with him.

He kept his gaze on her for several more seconds, then shot her a last gentle smile before heading upstairs and returning to work. She watched him go, exhaling lungfuls of stale air and inhaling fresh as she collapsed backward in her chair. Life was never going to be simple again, she thought wearily and with more than a hint of sadness.

His assurance that this trip would be devoted to business only made her feel more secure about making the arrangements and going along, but it still stung to know their heated, impulsive night together meant so little to him.

Not that she'd expected anything less. In truth, it's what she'd hoped for—that a single indiscretion wouldn't put her job or their friendship in jeopardy.

She couldn't be happier, she told herself; she'd gotten exactly what she wanted.

"William Dawson wants me to come to New York, look over his setup and give him some advice."

"I know, I've been telling him your schedule is full for a week now. If you want, I'll—"

"I've decided to go."

Her brows lifted at that. Only days ago, he'd been adamant that he wasn't interested in an out-of-town trip and told her to do whatever she needed to put off Dawson without alienating him as a client.

"All right," she said again, more slowly this time, "I'll make your plane and hotel reservations."

He gave a sharp nod. "Good. Make them for yourself, too. I want you to go along."

A shaft of panic speared her chest. Oh, no, she couldn't go with him. Just the two of them, on the plane, in the hotel when he wasn't meeting with William Dawson? No, that didn't sound like such a smart idea.

Taking a deep breath to reclaim her composure, she cleared her throat and said, "Thank you, but I'd rather not. There's more than enough work to be done here, and you've gone on plenty of these types of trips by yourself before. I'm sure you don't need me."

"Of course I do. Dawson is a big client. I want you there to help me charm him, but also to take notes and keep me in line. You know how distracted I get. I'll probably get up there, see what a mess his system is and offer to update it for free."

She gave a small snort. Peter wasn't quite that bad,

but probably close. When he saw something that needed to be done to a computer to bring it up to speed, he became almost entranced and lost sight of the fact that he was running a business and trying to make a living with his skills.

And he had been more distracted than usual lately. She'd found herself cleaning up after him and reminding him of daily tasks more often than in the past.

Of course, she couldn't blame him. She'd been feeling a little off her game, too, ever since letting her guard down in that elevator. They couldn't seem to find their stride again, regain the easy friendship and comfortable rapport that had made the workplace so peaceful in the past.

Curling her fingers into the palm of her hand, she fought the urge to reach out and stroke the firm line of his sculpted calf and pinned him with a sober glare. "You wouldn't be doing this just to get me alone, would you? Because we both know that night at the charity was a mistake and—"

He threw his head back and laughed loudly enough to startle her. "Are you kidding? That was ages ago," he said, waving a hand in dismissal. "This is business, Luce, and you're my right hand gal. I need you there. Besides, if I had any thoughts along those lines, we're alone now and are just about every day. I haven't tried to jump you yet, have I?"

Not giving her a chance to respond, he hopped off the desk and silently crossed the oriental carpet in his

sock-clad feet. At the archway, he stopped a his attention back to her. "So what do you say trust me enough to help me out on this? I'll pu at a great hotel," he added with a wink.

Tiny ripples of wariness caused her stomach to tract, but he looked and sounded so sincere, she fel most guilty for thinking he might be trying to trick h into going along.

Darting her tongue out to wet her suddenly dry lips, she tipped her head in acquiescence. "Fine, I'll make the arrangements. But I have to find someone to watch my cat before we can leave."

"That's right, you have a calico, don't you? Chocolate, Mocha…"

"Cocoa," she supplied, surprised he remembered that much about her personal life. And she didn't think he'd ever noticed the tiny framed photo tucked away on the far side of her computer monitor.

"Cocoa," he repeated. A warm smile curled the c ners of his mouth. "You'll have to introduce me so time."

She let that comment pass for a moment. "I leave her home alone and I'm not sure any of my fr will be available to check on her."

"How about a kennel or a pet sitter?"

She frowned slightly. "A pet sitter would be o long as she's reliable, but I won't even conside nel. Cocoa is much too skittish and set in her way never been out of my apartment, except to visit

But for some reason, her father's voice sounded in her head, warning her to *be careful what you wish for, you just might get it.*

Six

"**S**o let me get this straight. You were worried Lucy'd be pregnant from your night of hot sex in a hot elevator, but she isn't. Then you were afraid she'd misinterpret what happened between you and expect more of a relationship than you're ready for, but she didn't. And now you're making her go with you to New York on a so-called business trip with the flimsy excuse that you might need her to take notes, so *I* have to baby-sit her *cat*."

"It's a legitimate business trip," Peter said, doing his best to ignore Ethan's deep, animated scowl from the passenger seat of his sleek silver Infiniti.

"I think you're missing the point," his friend argued. "I've been relegated to a damn cat-sitter."

"What's the big deal? You like animals. And you do owe me for setting up the club's computer system and teaching your employees how to work the software."

A growl worked its way up from Ethan's throat. "I knew you'd make me pay for that, even though at the time, you claimed it was nothing. 'Just a friend helping a friend,'" he mimicked.

"That's right, and now I'm the friend who needs help."

Peter sighed, his fingers tapping nervously against the steering wheel as he drove in the direction of Lucy's apartment from The Hot Spot, where he'd picked up Ethan.

"Look, all you have to do is check in on Cocoa a couple of times a day, stick around for an hour or so to keep her company, if you can. You said yourself it wouldn't be a problem, and that you could get someone to cover for you at the club, if you needed. Lucy would really appreciate it, and I'll owe you one."

Ethan slouched down in his seat, crossing his arms over his chest. "You'll owe me more than one if the thing scratches or pees on me."

"It's a cat, Eth, not a rabid toddler. And you'd better not let Lucy hear you talking like that or make faces in front of her, or she'll call off the whole thing."

"You're that desperate to get into her pants again, huh?"

It was Peter's turn to glower. "I told you to not talk about her like that. I'm just looking for someone responsible and reliable to watch her cat while we're away."

"Just what I've always wanted to be—responsible and reliable." Ethan pouted.

"Oh, come on, you're a decent guy when you're not trying to charm some sweet young thing out of her thong panties."

Ethan grinned, flashing a row of sparkling white teeth. "Can I help it women find me irresistible?"

Peter rolled his eyes, but refrained from commenting, considering he needed Ethan in a good mood so he would do this favor for him. "Remember that when it comes to convincing Lucy you're head over heels about watching her cat, okay?"

"Hey, by the time I'm finished, she'll be asking you to watch the cat and me to whisk her away for a weekend of sweaty monkey sex."

The thought of the two of them together was so ridiculous, Peter nearly laughed out loud. But if there'd been a chance Ethan actually had a shot with Lucy, he'd be smiling around Peter's fist right this second.

He found a spot not far from Lucy's building and parked, then checked his watch. They had plenty of time for Ethan and Cocoa to get acquainted, Lucy to feel comfortable with the arrangements he'd made, and still get to the airport for their scheduled flight.

Lucy answered the door looking slightly flustered. "I'm almost ready," she said, waving them inside.

"Take your time," Peter offered.

She slipped back into the bedroom to finish packing, reappearing several minutes later.

With her bags by the door, she finally stopped moving long enough to take a breath and relax. "Thank you so much for doing this, Ethan. I know it can't be your first choice of ways to spend the better part of the week."

"Nonsense," he replied with his patented, full-points grin. "I'm happy to do it. This might even give me the chance to catch up on my stories. I just hope Cocoa likes soap operas."

Lucy's eyes narrowed cautiously and Peter cleared his throat, trying to warn Ethan that he might be laying it on a little thick.

Taking the hint, Ethan rubbed his hands together and glanced around the small kitchen. "So where is Cocoa, anyway? I'd like to meet her before you take off, see if she minds me staying with her for a while."

"She's afraid of strangers, which means she's probably hiding under the bed."

They moved in the direction of the bedroom, in search of the cat.

"You don't have to stay here the whole time, though," Lucy told Ethan. "She's used to me being gone a lot of the time for work. If you could just stop in once or twice a day to make sure she has enough food and water, that would be okay. I realize you need to be at the club at night, when I'd normally be home with her, but if you could stick around a while when you're here during the day, I'd really appreciate it. That way, she'll get some company and not feel quite so abandoned."

"No problem. Like I said, I'll watch some television, and Cocoa can sit on the couch with me, if she wants. At the very least, I'll keep up a steady stream of conversation so she knows someone is in the apartment with her."

Lucy beamed at that and Peter shook his head. Ethan in action was a sight to behold. No wonder women fell at his feet. Fifteen minutes ago, he'd been turning Peter's ears red with complaints about lowering himself to this task, and now he had Lucy gazing up at him like he was king of the damn universe.

If Peter hadn't known his friend was putting on an act for her benefit, he probably would have been annoyed. At the very least, he thought, he should be taking notes.

At the foot of the bed, made up with a thick safari comforter covered with lions, elephants and giraffes, Lucy got on her hands and knees and crouched down to peer beneath the raised bed frame.

"Cocoa, baby. Don't you want to come out and meet Ethan before Mommy leaves?"

Ethan's head lifted, one dark eyebrow quirked comically as he shot Peter a look that seemed to say, *You're sure this girl is sane, right?*

He nudged Ethan in the side with his elbow, afraid Lucy might look up and see the expression on his

Get FREE BOOKS and a FREE GIFT when you play the...

LAS VEGAS

GAME

Just scratch off the gold box with a coin. Then check below to see the gifts you get!

YES! I have scratched off the gold box. Please send me my **2 FREE BOOKS** and **gift for which I qualify.** I understand that I am under no obligation to purchase any books as explained on the back of this card.

326 SDL D7Y5   **225 SDL D7YV**

FIRST NAME   LAST NAME

ADDRESS

APT.#   CITY

STATE/PROV.   ZIP/POSTAL CODE   (S-D-06/05)

7	7	7	Worth TWO FREE BOOKS plus a BONUS Mystery Gift!
🍒	🍒	🍒	Worth TWO FREE BOOKS!
🔔	🔔	☘	TRY AGAIN!

www.eHarlequin.com

Offer limited to one per household and not valid to current Silhouette Desire® subscribers. All orders subject to approval.

▶ DETACH AND MAIL CARD TODAY! ▶

friend's face. And though Ethan might not be one to use baby talk to converse with another species, Peter knew his friend liked animals well enough and would take good care of Lucy's cat while they were away.

It was no less than he'd have expected of Lucy, though, to be so devoted to her pet. She was a caretaker, inside and out. Lord knew she took care of him better than anyone he'd ever known, including his own parents.

He wasn't surprised that she treated her cat like a child, the same way he wouldn't be at all amazed if she turned out to be the best mother in the world when she decided to have children of her own. Those kids and her family would come first above everything else.

Peter had never known love like that. His mother had tried, and he knew she loved him, but he'd always felt like an afterthought growing up. And he'd *never* been a priority in his father's life. For all the attention the old man had shown him, he might as well have not even existed.

Peter shook off the maudlin thoughts spiraling and multiplying in his brain like gnats when Lucy climbed to her feet, a fluffy ball of multicolored fur in her arms. The cat looked angry and put-out, her body arched, ears pressed flat against her head. But she let Ethan pet her with little more than a low growl from deep in her belly.

And Ethan, big, bad bully that he'd been in the car, seemed completely enraptured. He scratched the feline's ears and clicked his tongue. Peter thought he might even have cooed at one point. *Pushover.*

Once introductions were made and it was clear Cocoa and Ethan would get along like peas in a pod, Lucy showed him where everything was, gave him emergency phone numbers, then took a last glance around the small apartment before turning to Peter.

"All right, I think I'm ready."

He inclined his head, collecting her bags from near the door. "If you need anything," he told Ethan, "call us. You know where we're staying and you have my cell and pager numbers."

Ethan nodded, cat cradled under one arm like a football. "Have fun," he said, closing the door behind them.

Peter led Lucy out of the apartment building and across the street to his car, stowing her luggage in the trunk with his own. Once they were on the road, heading for the airport, Peter chanced a glance in her direction, noting the attractive but professional purple suit she'd worn to impress William Dawson, along with sleek high heels and dangling silver earrings.

"I hope Ethan meets your approval as a cat-sitter."

She tipped her head in his direction and gifted him with the ghost of a smile. "I like your friend. He's a bit of a smooth talker, but deep down, I think he's just an old softie. Cocoa will have him rolling around on the floor, dangling a string from his finger in no time."

"You're probably right." Peter chuckled, impressed that she'd pegged Ethan so quickly. Of course, his friend had been coming by the house ever since she started working for Peter, plying her with his good looks and playboy attitude.

Luckily Lucy had so far seemed immune to Ethan's advances. And Peter wasn't exactly the Hunchback of Notre Dame; he could hold his own with a group of pretty women—even up against Ethan. And especially where Lucy was concerned.

Ethan hadn't been completely right about his reasons for wanting Lucy along on this trip, but he hadn't been far off the mark, either. A part of him hoped they might end up making love again. He couldn't get the memory of being inside her out of his head, and if he got half the chance, he thought he would probably do his best to lure her back to his bed.

On the other hand, if she made it clear she wanted nothing more to do with him—at least in that respect— then he would have to take a step back and come to terms with her decision. He might not like it, but he would deal. And in a way, maybe it would be for the best.

But Lucy would have to be the one to throw her hands up and say no, because he honestly didn't think he had the strength to do it himself anymore. He wanted her too damn much.

Lucy turned slightly in her cozy, leather-upholstered business class seat, leaning against the plane's tiny rectangular window to watch Peter as he stowed his briefcase and her laptop computer in the overhead compartment. His broad chest and flat stomach rippled beneath the fine fabric of his shirt, pulling the material taut and making her mouth go dry.

Not for the first time, she wished she'd fought harder not to come along on this trip. It was too much to ask that she be required to work with him on a daily basis *and* travel out of town with him on business.

Sitting so close to him in the car on the drive to the airport, she'd felt like a sardine, stuffed into a tiny steel can next to the only other sardine who sent her pulse throbbing and her blood pressure skyrocketing out of control. And now she would be forced to endure the same type of conditions for the flight to New York.

Her stomach did a pitch and roll at the prospect. And then Peter settled into the seat beside hers, adjusted his seat belt, stretched his legs out in front of him, and Lucy thought she might have to reach for the airsick bag. Her poor nervous system was about to revolt.

Thankfully, the flight attendant came by then, asking if they'd like drinks before the plane took off. The woman smiled, her gaze lingering on Peter as she patted his shoulder and leaned so far over his seat, her breasts just about popped the front of her blue uniform.

Lucy was used to such blatant displays around Peter. Women flocked to him, and he usually flocked right back. The fact that he seemed oblivious to the flight attendant's current flirtations surprised her, but perhaps he was simply preoccupied by his upcoming business meetings.

"Excuse me." She cleared her throat and tried again, speaking more loudly until the blonde dragged her attention away from Peter. "Yes, I'd like a glass of Chardonnay, please." *A large one, and maybe later the bottle.* It was the only thing she could think of to slow her runaway heartbeat to a mere gallop.

It was small consolation, she supposed, that she wasn't alone in having this reaction to him. She was just the only one who'd apparently been driven to drink.

Once her wine and his scotch and soda had been delivered, they settled back in their seats to relax. Lucy noticed again that Peter took his drink and thanked the flight attendant, but otherwise ignored the woman's attempts to gain his masculine attention.

"What's the matter?" she asked, taking a sip from her glass. "Not interested in blondes this month?"

Peter shot her a confused glance. "What?"

"The flight attendant. She did everything but sit on your lap and wiggle."

His brows knit in a frown. "I don't know what you're talking about."

"Didn't you notice?" But to herself, she muttered, "That would be a first."

Over the rim of her glass, she saw Peter studying her intently. She knew she was being irrational and snippy, but she'd spent the past two years watching him parade around with one woman after another, and lately it felt like more than she could handle.

A tiny voice in the back of her head told her he

hadn't been hitting on the flight attendant. Hadn't even reacted to the woman's giggles or bounce. And as far as she knew, he hadn't been out—or in—with a single pretty girl since they'd been together. But that didn't seem to matter when the memory of dozens of other lovely young ladies were traipsing through her brain, getting her dander up.

"Are you angry with me, Lucy?"

"Of course not," she replied with a scoff, even though a part of her was.

"Then what's wrong? I've never seen you like this before. I've never seen you drink during a flight, either, let alone before we've gotten off the ground," he pointed out, flashing a look to the wine in her hand.

With a sigh, she placed the glass on the tray in front of her, then sat back in her seat and turned to face him more fully.

"I'm sorry," she said, the wind going out of her sails. "It's just…Don't you ever think about the future? About having more than the flavor of the month to warm your bed?"

Eyes widening, Peter shifted uncomfortably but didn't break the visual hold he had on her. With a nervous chuckle, he wanted to know, "What brought this on?"

She shook her head, unwilling to answer, since the first thing that flashed across her mind was an image of the two of them, on the floor of a hotel elevator, making love.

"I guess I'd have to say no," Peter murmured, his lips thinning. "I try very hard not to think about the future, except where business is concerned."

"Why not?"

If possible, his mouth compressed more tightly, the sides sliding down into a frown. "It's better not to spend too much time contemplating things that can never be."

A ripple of sadness flowed outward from the region of her heart at such a grim declaration.

"I'm not sure I understand what you mean," she said carefully. "Are you suffering from some dread disease I don't know about and only have a few months left to live? Or maybe you're sterile and can't have children, so there's no point in contemplating marriage."

Peter whipped his head around to see if anyone was listening in on their conversation. "Jeez, Luce, talk a little louder, why don't you. I don't think the people in row twenty-three heard you." Then he grew serious. "I'm not sterile and I'm not dying. At least not that I know of. But let's face it, there's no such thing as happily-ever-after, and I'd be a terrible husband and father even if there were."

Lucy stared at him, incredulous, so many thoughts whirling around in her brain, she could barely make sense of them. *Bad husband, no happily-ever-after, things that can never be. What* was he talking about? And how had he come up with such outlandish notions?

Granted, they'd only known each other for two

years, but if he'd ever been married, she thought she'd
have heard about it by now. Some brief mention of an
ex-wife or whispered rumors about why the marriage
hadn't worked out.

"I'm sorry," she managed once she'd blinked and re-
gained some of the moisture in her suddenly dry mouth,
"but you're going to have to elaborate. Why in heaven's
name would you think you'd make a bad husband and
father?"

"Genetics don't lie."

"Genetics," she repeated, still not understanding.
She felt as though he was speaking another language,
with none of the words finding definitions in her limited vocabulary.

"I take it you've never heard me talk about my father."

She searched her memory, but couldn't recall a single time he'd spoken to her about his parents, and only
now began to think that fact odd.

Not waiting for an answer, he continued. "My father
was a real son of a bitch. A shark in the business world,
and well respected for it, but as a husband and father,
he stank. I don't know why he bothered getting married at all, and I think I must have been conceived either by immaculate conception or in a moment of
extreme weakness.

"Throughout my entire childhood, I don't think I
ever heard him say a kind word to my mother or saw
her smile when he was around. We didn't go on outings

or spend quality time together. We didn't even have meals as a family, or if we did, they were eaten in relative silence, with my father hurrying through so he could rush off to another business meeting or lock himself in his study to work."

Peter held himself rigid, as though barring against any hint of emotion that might seep past the bitterness and resentment. Her heart ached for him, for the little boy he'd been, starving for his father's affection and getting none.

"What about your mother?" she inquired softly. "Was she good to you?"

He responded with a careless shrug. "She did her best, tried to compensate for my father's absence. But she was distracted by it herself, always trying to keep him home, give him reasons to spend time with us."

Lucy wanted to wrap her arms around him and offer comfort, hug him tight for all the times in his childhood when he'd been ignored or pushed aside or made to feel like less than the most important thing in the world to the two people who should have loved him above everyone and everything else in their lives.

"And because your father wasn't very good at marriage and family, you've automatically decided you won't be, either. Is that right?"

"Does an apple fall far from the tree?" His mouth twisted, the question dripping with cynicism.

"Peter." She stopped, worrying the inside of her lip, unsure how to go on. There was so much she wanted to say to him, so many fallacies she wanted to lay to rest. But her mind was a jumble of facts and feelings. She knew if she said the wrong thing, Peter would clam up, curling in on himself to once again hide the little boy who had been hurt and disillusioned at such a young age.

"You can't believe that," she whispered. "Not really."

The expression on his face, though, told her he did—unequivocally.

The engines of the plane turned over then, making it harder to be heard over the loud, humming whir. Crossing her legs in his direction, she leaned closer so she wouldn't have to raise her voice, laying a hand on his arm. Beneath her fingers, the muscles bunched and tensed as he clutched the metal armrest.

"Peter, your father was distant and uncaring, and I'm sorry for that. I don't think anyone would argue the fact that neither of your parents did right by you. But you're not a clone of your father, you're your own man. That's the beauty of children; they can grow up wiser than their parents and learn not to make the same mistakes as previous generations."

She squeezed his arm and brushed the back of her hand lovingly along the line of his jaw. She knew she should play it safe and walk away. Accept his reasoning and count herself fortunate not to have gotten too heavily involved with his personal demons.

But she was already emotionally invested in this

man. Her heart had been engaged soon after she started working for him, and she was only more soundly entrenched now that he'd shared a part of his past with her.

"I happen to think you'd make a wonderful husband and father," she told him earnestly. "You're kind and generous and patient, and have a great sense of humor. Any woman would be lucky to have you, and your children—if you ever have them—will think you hung the moon and the stars."

Seven

Lucy's words penetrated deep into his soul, warming a place he'd thought long dead. He only wished he could believe them.

A part of him wanted to…so badly, he felt a burning sensation at the backs of his eyes. He turned his head and blinked quickly, taking a moment to catch his breath and steady his out of control emotions.

But you couldn't rewrite history, and he knew what happened when a man tried to have a wife and family while also trying to build and maintain a thriving business. One would suffer, and if his own upbringing was any indication, it would likely be the family. That was a risk he couldn't—*wouldn't*—take.

"I wish I could believe that," he rasped, turning his arm over and twining her fingers with his own when they slid into his palm. "But I've had too much experience with the other side of the coin. I learned early on that a person can either concentrate on his job, his corporate image, or he can concentrate on his family—he can't have both. And I'm sorry, Lucy, but Reyware is too important to me to let anything interfere. My entire focus right now is on getting the company off the ground and well into the black. Maybe later, when I'm older and Reyware is stable enough to put others in charge…maybe then I'll take a chance on a wife and kids. For now, though, I can't put someone—adult or child—through what my father put my mom and me through."

"You only think that way because it's all you've ever known," Lucy pointed out gently. "If you'd grown up differently, you might have a dozen kids by now."

He wrinkled his nose at her wild supposition. "I'm only thirty-two, Luce. How is that even possible?"

She shot him a cheeky grin. "Well, maybe not a full dozen, but if you'd gotten started early, you could be close."

His expression must have still looked doubtful because she adjusted her weight until her shoulder and the full length of her arm rested firmly against his.

"Let me tell you about my family," she said, a wealth of warmth and affection clear in her affectionate tone.

"My father is a civil engineer. He's been at the same

company for twenty-five years, beginning as a low-level assistant and working his way up to Vice President. My mother has worked as an elementary teacher all her life. They met in college, got married right after graduation, and had my brother, Adam, before their first anniversary. I came next, and then Jessica. Both of my parents worked full-time through all of our childhoods, but I don't ever remember a time when they weren't there for us. We sat at the dining-room table every night for dinner, shared the day's events. We went on picnics and took vacations, played checkers and board games and Frisbee, went to the beach and the community pool. Some of the best times of my life were spent with Mom, Dad, Adam, and Jess. I can't wait to get married and start a family of my own so I can recapture some of that early happiness and show my own children how it feels to be loved and adored, unconditionally."

With the hand he wasn't holding in a near-death grip, she patted his knee. "Now, do you want to tell me again that a man can't be a successful entrepreneur and doting father at the same time? My father certainly managed well enough, and my brother is following firmly in his footsteps."

He understood what she was trying to say and envied her blissful, storybook upbringing. But it still sounded like a fairy tale to him. And in his life, was every bit as fictional.

"I'm glad you have happy memories of your childhood," he told her judiciously, "and that your parents were able to find time for the three of you, given their busy schedules. But your father and brother obviously come from different stock than the men in my family. For me, it's just not possible, the same as it wasn't possible for my father or his father."

When Peter cocked his head and met her gaze, he saw the sadness and sympathy in her eyes, and almost resented it. With a sigh, she loosened her fingers from his grasp and uncrossed her legs, moving back to her own side of the roomy, first-class leather seats.

Retrieving her glass of wine, she took a healthy sip and then said, "I hope you're wrong, Peter. I truly, truly do. Because you deserve to be a husband and father, and to prove yourself wrong."

They arrived at the downtown Manhattan hotel a few hours later, tired and uncomfortable from the tack their conversation had taken on the plane. After that, they'd barely spoken unless necessary.

For her part, Lucy found herself distracted by Peter's confession and the picture he'd painted of his childhood. It explained so much about him.

Why he dated beautiful but vacuous women with no thought past the night they'd spend in his bed. Or the ones obviously interested in little more than his money, whom he seemed to use and discard as easily as yesterday's newspaper.

It suddenly all made perfect sense. He surrounded himself with people who wouldn't expect too much of him, wouldn't pressure him to make promises. Because the idea of committing to anything more permanent than a goldfish scared Peter straight down to his boxer shorts.

Which might also be why, up until that Friday night in the elevator at the Four Seasons, he'd never made a single move on her. Never seemed to notice her feminine existence, let alone the hints she dropped to let him know she wouldn't turn him down if he did.

And now, she wasn't sure how to feel. She'd spent so long being half in love with him, and then getting to experience the long-awaited, earth-shattering sensation of making love with him, that she found it hard to let go of the fantasy she'd built in her mind.

Given his strong aversion to marriage and family, however, she would probably be better off setting her sights on someone a bit more attainable. Like Mel Gibson or Brad Pitt.

Peter desperately wanted to avoid the ties and responsibilities of marriage and children, and though Lucy thought a few stern arguments or hours on a therapist's couch would go a long way toward relieving him of his adolescent burden, the fact was she *did* want those things.

She'd grown up in a happy home, with two loving parents, and someday she hoped to create those same qualities for her own kids. For a time, she'd even let herself imagine she would have that life and those children with Peter. Now she knew she would have better luck teaching Cocoa to bark like a guard dog.

Watching him from the corner of her eye as he checked them in at the front desk, she had the sudden urge to put her head down on the countertop and weep. It was such a waste. Like many women, she'd often joked that all the good men were either gay or married. Now she realized the best of those men was highly allergic to any sign of a serious relationship.

Sliding the key cards into his jacket pocket, Peter picked up both their carry-on bags and started toward the bank of elevators on the far side of the elegant lobby. Lucy followed at a more sedate pace, swallowing the mild nausea that threatened from the day's keen disappointments.

The ride to the tenth floor passed in relative silence, soft instrumental music filling the small space and spurring the start of a headache just behind her eyes. She remembered the last time they'd been alone together in a hotel elevator…

Her inner muscles clenched at the very thought as heat rushed over her, and for a moment she wished for another city-wide power outage. Ten minutes when the rest of the world would disappear and they could once again find complete, satisfied abandon in each other's arms.

But then the doors slid open and reality returned. The lights stayed on, Peter's breathing remained steady, and there was no repeat performance of the wild lovemaking they'd shared before.

Lucy couldn't decide whether to be happy or sad

about that, but she let Peter open the door to her suite and usher her inside. She crossed the room, flipping on lights as she went and opening the heavy drapes to reveal a panoramic view of the city. Tall gray buildings obscured the skyline while cars filled the streets below like ants trailing away from a picnic buffet.

Behind her, Peter set her overnight bag on the bed and moved toward the door that connected their two rooms. "We're meeting Dawson for dinner in the hotel restaurant at seven," he reminded her.

She checked the watch at her wrist, then turned her head a fraction, taking in his sandy blond hair and suit, both slightly rumpled from the trip. It took every ounce of will in her body not to offer to iron his jacket and slacks or otherwise help him get ready for his meeting. But with only half an hour until they were supposed to get together with William Dawson, she needed every spare moment to freshen up.

"I'll be ready," she said.

He stood there a second longer, looking like he might say something. Then he stepped through the connecting door and closed it quietly behind him.

This was good, she thought. Getting back to business, putting their relationship back on a professional footing. It might not be what she'd been hoping for, for the past two years, but now that she knew about his deep-rooted aversion to anything permanent, it was better for her to wrap her mind around the fact that Peter was not the marrying kind.

And since she wasn't in the market for a man to simply warm her bed or fill her life on a temporary basis, she needed to get it through her head that Peter Reynolds was off her short list.

It wasn't the end of the world. There were other men out there, ones who wouldn't be quite as apprehensive of the "M" word or the idea of settling down and starting a family.

Maybe it was time to seek some of them out.

Peter scowled, his brows dipping so low, they almost completely obliterated his vision.

What the hell did she think she was doing? And who the hell had told her to pack a dress like that, anyway?

Lucy sat across the table from him, entirely too close to William Dawson, laughing loudly and hanging on the man's every word. And Dawson, in return, was practically drooling on Lucy.

This was supposed to be a business dinner, but she'd changed from her classy purple suit to a low-cut, high-hemmed cocktail dress. Black, with flowered and filigree lace at the edges, which left much too much of her arms and neck and legs and chest bare for Peter's peace of mind.

She'd come with him in a secretarial capacity, but she acted as though she was on a date—with Dawson, no less. And they had yet to discuss Dawson's company or the plans he had for Peter's involvement. The man seemed content to bask in Lucy's feminine attention, and she, in turn, seemed determined to work Will into a lather.

But if she thought she could send Peter back up to the hotel rooms and take off on Dawson's arm to spend the evening doing God knows what, she had another think coming.

If she spent the night with anyone, it would be Peter. And if she wound up in anyone's bed, it would be his, not Will Dawson's. He didn't care how much she was flirting or how receptive the man obviously was.

Lucy laughed again at something Will said and Peter felt his blood pressure spike. One more suggestive joke or over-the-top giggle and he thought he might snap. He'd shatter the wine glass in his hand or drive the tines of his fork into his former friend's fingers where they covered and wrapped around Lucy's atop the linen tablecloth.

"Don't you think we should get down to business?" he finally said, the words rumbling from his throat in something close to a growl.

Both Lucy and Will cocked their heads, glancing at him for the first time in more than an hour, as though they'd forgotten he was even present at the same table.

Untangling their twined arms and hands, Lucy sat back a bit in her chair, away from Will and gave a small smile.

"Of course," she murmured. "I'm sorry, I didn't mean to distract you from your purpose." She pulled a small legal pad and pen from her handbag, poised to take notes. "Please, go on. I'm ready when you are."

Peter felt a punch to his gut as powerful as any an opponent could have delivered in a title fight. He had used the excuse of needing her along as his assistant to manipulate her into coming, and now she was throwing her notepad down like a gauntlet. Showing him she knew her place, reminding him of their professional arrangement, and all but spelling out that their conversation on the plane meant if he wasn't open to marriage and family, then she wasn't open to him.

He'd known that. Even as he was relating facts from his childhood to her, he'd known that she would take it to mean he wasn't interested in developing anything of a permanent nature with her.

Lucy had grown up very differently than he, and though she may not be on the hunt for a husband right this minute, he knew she had visions of picket fences and two-point-three kids running through her brain. He might be fun to have as a lover for the short term, but he would either have to let her go or turn into a long-term kind of guy right quick. And knowing he never intended to marry or reproduce meant she'd likely knocked him off her list completely the minute he'd admitted as much.

A little voice in the back of his brain cheered. He should be happy, relieved, grateful she'd cut off any chances of an ongoing relationship. That way, he would never have to worry that she'd begin to expect more from him than he was willing to give. He'd never have to prepare a speech for letting her down easy or explain why she might share his bed, but would never share his life. He would never have to see her tears or listen to her wails as she stormed out of his house and cursed him for wasting her time.

Been there, done that.

So why, instead, was his stomach churning, his upper lip sweating? Why was there a sharp pain in the region of his heart?

Because he was a sap, that's why. Ridiculous to think it could be more than a fanciful notion of keeping Lucy with him forever. As anything other than his assistant, at least.

Maybe he'd been watching too many chick flicks lately or leaving the television on the wrong channel while he worked. Whatever the cause of his recent bout of melancholia, he was damn certain he didn't plan to change his lifelong goals and beliefs just because he'd spent one night in an overheated elevator car with Lucy. Best sex of his life or not, no woman was worth running the risk of turning into his father, of irreparably ruining multiple lives.

Refusing to meet Lucy's gaze or the censure written there, he shifted his focus instead to Will and steered the conversation back where it belonged—firmly on the business at hand.

Lucy didn't know what had crawled up Peter's butt and died, but about halfway through dinner, he'd turned surly and cross. He'd discussed William Dawson's company and the software system he thought best for the man's growing business, but he'd been so curt about it that he might have been a rival CEO in the center of a corporate takeover.

And darned if Lucy could figure out why. Before they'd left Georgetown for New York, Peter had given the impression that he and Will were friends, as well as associates. They were roughly the same age, had grown up with similar backgrounds, and were both building personal companies they hoped would be successful.

So why was Peter suddenly acting as if Will had stolen his favorite toy?

Unless Lucy's behavior during the meal had set him off.

Her cheeks flushed as she remembered, and she admitted to herself that she might have gone a touch overboard.

Once she'd made the decision to go in search of an eligible man—or men—her seductive side had come out full-force. Will Dawson was an attractive, unattached man. The minute they'd walked into the hotel restaurant and Peter had introduced them, she'd detected a note of interest in the man's dark eyes and decided to see where it led.

It had led rather quickly to a lot of laughter, a few fluttered eyelashes, and some tentative touching of both hands and legs beneath the table.

Lucy hadn't realized Peter noticed, let alone that her actions would bother him. After all, he'd made it clear immediately following their one night together that it had been a mistake and he didn't intend to let it happen again. Then, on the plane, he'd gone even further by telling her a bit about his childhood and assuring her he never intended to settle down with anyone, not even her.

So why shouldn't she be allowed to date other men? Even those of Peter's acquaintance. Even in his presence. He wasn't her brother or father, with some overblown sense of familial protection that allowed him to tell her who she could see or flirt with. She was a grown woman, looking forward to a happy future that would hopefully someday include a husband and children. And if Peter wasn't willing to give her those things, then he had no right to keep her from them, either.

As she strolled across the hotel room, stripping out of her dress and stockings, Lucy couldn't decide whether to be amused or angry by the entire situation. Peter was the man she wanted, but he didn't want her. And yet, it seemed he also didn't want her to be with anyone else.

Well, he couldn't have it both ways. She'd spent the past two years fawning over him, believing he might one day sit up and take notice of her, and that they might have a future together. Now that she knew that wasn't the case, she wanted to get on with her life.

She thought of Will, with his short black hair, set in glossy spikes along his head with a touch of gel. His chocolate-brown eyes and easy smile. She might have invited him upstairs after dinner if Peter hadn't been all but shooting daggers and chewing glass.

A second later, though, as she reached into the shower to turn on the water, she knew that wasn't true. She might have invited Will up to her room, but she doubted anything would have happened. For one, she wasn't the kind of girl to sleep with a man she barely knew the first night they met. For another, she was afraid she wouldn't be able to banish Peter from her mind long enough to be intimate with somebody else.

Stepping under the warm spray, she let water sluice down her body, wet her hair. It felt wonderful, and for the first time all night, she let herself relax completely, let the tension wash away from her muscles as easily as the shampoo and soap suds slid down the drain.

She stayed in the shower longer than usual, until steam fogged the glass of the bathroom mirror and her skin turned warm and silky. Then she wrapped one towel around her hair and another around her body, tucking the corner between her breasts to hold it fast.

While she was still damp, she squeezed a dollop of sweet-smelling moisturizer into the palm of her hand and smoothed it over her arms and legs, then patted herself dry. With the floral scent of lotion filling the small room, she combed and blow-dried her hair before opening the door and stepping out into the rest of the hotel room.

Letting the towel from around her body drop at the foot of the king size bed, she took the three strides to the dresser in the nude and dug a nightie out of the top drawer. The emerald satin slipped on over her head, settling its spaghetti straps over her shoulders and lace bodice along her breasts with a gentle whoosh.

A throat clearing across the room spun Lucy around with a startled yip. Peter sat in the corner, slouched down in a chair, hidden by shadows.

"Good Lord," she breathed, "you scared me half to death."

It was a testament to how comfortable she felt with him that she didn't even realize she'd just pranced in front of him completely naked for a full minute. When she did, she gave another yelp and grabbed for her earlier discarded bath towel.

"Peter!" she chastised, using the white terry cloth to cover herself from neck to knee, even though she was now more than adequately dressed in the short, slinky nightgown. "What are you doing here? How did you get in?"

He cocked his head in the direction of the connecting door. "It was unlocked. I wanted to talk to you, but I didn't expect you to be walking around naked." Sitting up a bit straighter, he had the decency to look abashed. "Sorry."

For the first time since sending her heart into overdrive with his sudden appearance, she noticed the condition of his suit, wrinkled and disheveled. His tie had been loosened and draped down his chest at an odd angle, and it looked as though he'd run his fingers through his hair a few thousand times.

Her embarrassment faded, replaced by concern, and she moved to sit on the corner of the bed nearest his chair.

"Is something wrong?" she asked.

For a moment, he didn't answer. Then he bent forward, resting his elbows on his thighs, hands clasping and unclasping between his parted knees as he hung his head dejectedly.

"I came to apologize for dinner. I acted like an ass."

Lucy crossed her legs, letting the towel fall to her lap. "You were a little asslike," she agreed softly.

He lifted his head and gave her a small smile. "You noticed that, huh?"

"I noticed. I'm just not sure what came over you. I thought you and Will were friends."

"We are, at least as far as business goes."

"Then why did you treat him so shabbily? And me, too, for that matter."

"Truth?" He slanted an uneasy glance in her direction. "I didn't like the way he was looking at you, touching you. Or the way you reacted to him."

Setting the still-damp towel aside, she scooched another inch toward the edge of the mattress. "Why, Peter? Why do you care what I do or who I do it with? It's not like you're interested, not judging by what you said on the plane."

In one fluid motion, Peter abandoned his chair. Towering above her, he leaned in, fists digging into the bedspread on either side of her hips until their noses nearly touched.

"That's where you're wrong," he whispered, his voice low and rough, running over her like a sheet of sandpaper. "Because I am interested. God help me, but I am."

Eight

Desire stabbed through Peter, and the closer he got to Lucy, the sharper that desire became. Going down on one knee in front of her, he breathed in the clean, shampooed fragrance of her long, black hair, let his gaze roam over the rosy glow of her shower-fresh skin.

"I tried to deny it," he said, the words ripped from his throat as he stared up at her, blood pounding in his veins. "That one night was supposed to be just that—one night. One night when I finally got to experience what I'd been dreaming of since the first time you came to interview for the job as my assistant. One night when things got a bit crazy and my claustrophobia served as the perfect excuse to taste your lips, caress your body, feel you move beneath me while we made love."

He lifted a hand to her face, stroked the back of his fingers over the baby-soft silk of her cheek. "I hoped that would be enough, for both of us. Because I can't give you what you need, what you deserve. You want it all—a wedding, babies, happily ever after. And I want those things for you, but I can't be the one to give them to you. Not now, maybe not ever."

Letting his hand dip lower, he traced the line of her jaw, the slender column of her neck, the gentle slope of her chest. The lacy front of her liquid green gown exposed all but the very tips of her breasts. They drew his eye and then his touch.

"Seeing you tonight, though, flirting with Will... There were a couple of times during dinner when I had to stop myself from leaping across the table and choking him with his napkin."

His hold shifted from below the curve of her breasts to her waist and squeezed. "Tell me to leave, Lucy," he implored, meeting her ocean-blue eyes. "Say you hate me and never want to see me again. Kick me out before I do something really stupid like beg you to go to bed with me."

Lucy raised an arm, feathering her manicured fingers through the hair at his temple. "I don't hate you," she murmured. "And you don't have to beg."

Lowering her head, she pressed her lips to his, her hands spreading across his cheeks and neck. Her mouth felt like molten lava flowing from an active volcano. Heat poured through his veins, all but giving off steam, bringing every hormone in his body to full attention.

Coming up on his knees, he started to stand, only to push her back on the mattress. The satiny fabric of her nightie rode high on her thighs as he hovered over her, mouth devouring, hands exploring.

He'd missed this the first time around. Watching her, seeing her beautiful hair spilled out around her like a halo, her eyes turn dark with passion, her nipples pearl at the tips of her pert breasts. And it was a damn shame, because every inch of her was so beautiful, his teeth ached.

He stroked her shoulders and arms, memorized the shape of her womanly form with its hills and valleys, dips and swells. Electricity sparked at his fingertips as they skimmed across her flesh, sending the sensations straight to his groin.

A moan rolled up from his diaphragm as their tongues tangled and twisted. Her legs wrapped around his like vines, and he could feel the silk of her skin even through the material of his dress slacks.

The nails on one of Lucy's hands dug into his back while the other loosened the knot of his tie. Tossing it aside, she moved to the buttons of his shirt while he rocked his hips into the cradle of her thighs and skimmed a hand beneath the hem of her gown.

With each movement of their bodies, he slid Lucy farther and farther up the length of the mattress, until her head was propped on the pillows. The new position gave them more than enough room to spread out and enjoy themselves.

As soon as she'd finished with the buttons, he shrugged out of both the white shirt and gray suit jacket, letting them fall to the floor. He began inching her gown upwards, over her hips, her torso. Lucy raised her arms so he could slide the slinky material off completely.

She lay beneath him, blessedly naked. Sexier and more lovely, if possible, than when she'd stepped out of the bathroom after her shower and dropped the towel. And this time, he didn't have to just sit back and watch, he could touch and taste and stroke to his heart's content.

Her fingers at his waist succeeded in unhooking his belt, then shifted to the button and zipper of his pants. When both slid free, she tunneled her fingers inside, into the band of his briefs and pushed everything down past his hips.

He groaned as she raked her nails across the sensitive flesh of his buttocks and the backs of his thighs, then quickly kicked off his shoes and shrugged out of his slacks and underwear. Stretching out atop her, their heated bodies molded together. Hard on soft, rough against smooth, they fit like pieces of a puzzle, creating a picture that felt…right. Unbearably perfect, even if it was only temporary.

He used his lips and teeth to graze her collarbone, working his way down to her breasts. With light, butterfly kisses, he circled the pert, plum-colored areolas, then eased closer, blowing lightly on the tight flesh, letting his tongue dart out to lick her pointed nipples.

"You smell delicious," he murmured against her moist skin. "Like strawberries and cream."

She gave a breathy chuckle. "It's flowers. Rose soap and honeysuckle shampoo."

"Whatever it is," he said, "you smell good enough to eat."

He dug his teeth into the cushiony side of her breast, then licked away the sting with this tongue. Continuing the onslaught, he suckled one breast while kneading the other with his palm until Lucy writhed beneath him, arching her back and twisting her hips. Little sounds, like a mewling kitten, rolled past her lips, urging him on.

"Unfair," she whispered. And then she slipped a hand between them, reaching down to stroke the long, hard length of his erection. It pulsed in her hand and sent fireworks bursting behind his closed eyelids.

"That's better," she told him. "Now you know how I feel. How you *make* me feel."

With a growl, he yanked her legs up and over his shoulders, switching his attention from her breasts to her ribcage. He kissed a ring around her belly button, a path across her abdomen, and then lightly nuzzled the springy curls at the vee of her thighs. She moaned in protest, pushing at his shoulders to dislodge him, but he held firm.

"Hush," he ordered against her womanhood. "Let me. I've been dreaming of this longer than you can imagine."

She seemed to relax then, her head sinking into the pillow, her ankles crossing in the middle of his back. He licked her like a cat, tasting the musky sweetness that was her own intimate flavor.

Lucy hummed with pleasure as his tongue lapped and explored. Her pelvis rose and fell, begging for completion. And he gave it to her, deepening his attentions, focusing on the tiny bud of desire that made her squirm. Her breathing began to come in pants, shorter and louder, until her spine bowed and she screamed in ecstasy.

Peter felt the orgasm vibrate through her body and into his own, arousing him even more. He couldn't wait to be inside her again, to feel that heat, that wet, that sense of completeness he'd never experienced before in his life.

Only with Lucy.

Only when he shut off his brain and let himself enjoy the spell she wove around them. Without thinking of all the reasons they wouldn't work, all the ways he could hurt her.

Her legs slid from his shoulders, boneless and limp. He took the opportunity to crawl back up her long, lithe frame to her lips, drawing them into his mouth one at a time.

"Thank you," he whispered against her cheek. "That was amazing."

Her eyes opened to slits, looking droopy and satisfied. She tried to laugh, but it came out as more of an amused wheeze.

"I should be thanking you. It *was* amazing. And you didn't even get to have any fun yet." Her fingers combed through his hair and a soft smile crested her lips.

"Oh, I had fun, believe me. Watching you come, knowing I brought you to that point, is the single most incredible event of my life. Not counting the little escapade in the elevator, since I couldn't see you. Or anything that might come next, which I'm guessing will be equally remarkable."

"I don't know," she said with a teasing grin, still stroking his scalp. "What we've already done was pretty out-of-this-world, at least for me. I'm not sure anything could top it. Maybe we should just quit while we're ahead."

"Oh, no." Peter dug his teeth into the taut flesh between neck and shoulder, branding her with his mark. "We're just getting started. Before the night is over, I intend to make you scream at least six or eight more times."

"Six or eight, hmm? That's quite a bar you're setting for yourself. Are you sure you can handle it?"

He gazed down at her, feigning irritation with what he hoped was a devilishly raised brow. "*I* can handle it. The question is, can you?"

She drew her legs up and encircled his waist, bringing him that much closer to the entrance of her femininity. The damp warmth dusting his throbbing erection made him clench his teeth to keep from popping like a bottle of champagne right then and there.

Her low voice washed over him, full of sensual promises. "I'm certainly willing to try."

He rested his forehead against her brow, then placed a light kiss on the tip of her nose. "This time, we're going to be more careful," he told her.

Rolling slightly away, he reached to the floor for his earlier discarded pants. He dug his wallet out of the back pocket and a condom out of the wallet.

"I've been carrying this with me ever since our encounter in the elevator, just in case."

"Do you only have the one?"

Pulling himself back up on the bed, he shot her a pirate's grin, then ripped the foil-lined packet open with his teeth. "Unfortunately, yes. But I'll run down to the hotel gift shop for another box before we need them."

"Mmm, a man with a plan. What a turn-on."

He chuckled as he took the condom from its wrapper and moved to sheath himself. But her hand stopped him, taking the latex circle from his grasp.

"Let me."

Lowering her feet to the mattress, Lucy shimmied toward the headboard, getting to her knees. Peter did the same, until they were kneeling on the bed, face-to-face. She skimmed a palm down the broad expanse of his chest, marveling at the play of muscles. How they defined his sculpted, mouthwatering form and rippled beneath her touch.

Her own stomach clenched in anticipation as she leaned forward and kissed first one flat male nipple and then the other. He shuddered in response.

His reaction made her bold…not that she hadn't already been more daring than usual with him. But that's what Peter did to her. He made her feel powerful and uninhibited. Womanly and wanton.

"Lie back," she ordered, advancing on him and pushing firmly on his pectorals.

He followed her instructions, going flat on his back across the bunched and slippery hotel-issue bedspread. She straddled him, crawling up his long, rough-haired legs until she could rest her bottom high on his thighs.

He watched her through thick blond lashes, his hands moving to cup her hips. "You're trying to kill me, aren't you?"

Lucy shook her head. Her hair fanned out in a black veil and fell around her shoulders. "Just a little death."

The air left his lungs in a hiss. "Very funny. If you're not careful, it could be a big one, and maybe the real thing."

She bent over, letting her belly come in contact with his pointing erection. It pressed like steel into her flesh, even though the surface felt like crushed velvet.

His chest rose and fell with his heavy breathing. Hovering just above his parted lips, she exhaled, letting her warm breath caress his mouth and cheeks. "You're not afraid of a little pleasure, are you?"

"A little?" he spoke raggedly. "No. But with you,

there's no chance of 'a little.' It's going to be a lot, and it's going to be phenomenal…if I make it that far."

"If you don't make it all the way the first time," she teased wickedly, "we'll just have to try, try again."

Peter groaned, deep in his throat, and his hips arched off the bed almost of their own volition. A shock of awareness shot through her at the action, and suddenly she didn't want to play anymore. She only wanted him inside her, pounding and thrusting until their teeth rattled and their minds turned to mush.

Lifting up again, she took hold of his arousal with one hand at the base while she situated the condom over the tip with the other. She felt his entire body tense under her and wasted no time rolling the protection into place.

His fingers dug into her buttocks as she repositioned herself and began taking his hot length into her body. Inch by inch, she eased down. He pulsed inside her, seeming to grow larger even as she engulfed him.

When she was fully seated, they both released heartfelt sighs.

"That's a pretty good start," he muttered.

"And it's bound to get even better, right?"

"God, I hope so."

Flattening both palms on his ribcage, she rose up on her knees a fraction, letting him slide partially out of her body even as she tightened her internal grip to keep him in place. He bit his bottom lip, stifling a moan, and she moved back down.

Then she arched forward and repeated the motion. Up. Down. Back. Forth. Side to side. She changed direction with each stroke, keeping him on edge. His hands clutched her hips, clenching and unclenching as he lifted off the mattress, thrusting upwards to reach her.

Her fingers curled against his firm abdomen like talons as heat lightning raced through her. Tension spiraled at her center, growing tighter and tighter until every muscle in her body grew tightrope taut and her lungs froze in her chest.

Ecstasy rolled over her in a waterfall of sensation, sharp at first and then warm and comforting. Beneath her, Peter's lips curled back from his gritted teeth as he flexed his hips one last time and climaxed inside her.

They floated back down to earth slowly, hearts pounding, bones the consistency of vanilla pudding. She fell across him, limp and sated. Her hair covered them like a blanket, hiding her eyes and getting in her mouth, but she didn't care.

She'd never felt anything in her life even close to what she'd just experienced. The things Peter did to her, the heights and emotions he wrung from her. He played her like a well-tuned instrument, and she sang in response.

His chest rose and fell as he struggled to draw air into his lungs, and his heart beat erratically under her ear. Both made her feel safe, as though she never needed to move again. She could die right here, right now, and not suffer a single regret.

Her eyelids were too heavy to open when he smoothed a hand over the back of her head. She purred in contentment, but remained wilted.

"Are you okay?" he asked, his mouth moving against her temple.

Her only answer was a noncommittal grunt.

He chuckled, the sound vibrating along both their bodies. "Well, I have to say I'm surprised the bed held up. Halfway through, I expected the springs to give out and the two of us to find ourselves on the floor."

"Halfway through, I'm surprised you could think at all," she muttered lazily. "But the floor might not be a bad idea for the next time around."

"God, I love a woman who plans for the future."

He shifted, sending aftershocks of desire through her lower regions where they were still intimately connected. With a small groan, he rolled to his side, depositing her on her back on the mattress and kissing her brow.

"I just need to take care of this," he said, sitting up on the edge of the bed and removing the used condom. He made his way to the bathroom, closing the door all but a crack behind him.

Lucy lay there as the seconds ticked by, staring up at the ceiling. It was too much effort to move, though she knew she should. And Peter's last words were humming through her brain, sending nerve endings that were previously numb with pleasure into unpleasant awareness.

Love. He'd used the word, but he didn't mean it…not the way she wished he would.

A part of her knew she shouldn't be upset. She should shrug off his comment as the simple turn of phrase it had been. But another part of her was reminded in living color of the problems that still stood between them.

Great sex was one thing…if they handed out awards for outstanding performances in the bedroom, Peter would have a wall full of gold medals. With him, she might even win a few of her own.

She'd let herself pretend nothing else mattered for the chance to be with him again, but the fact remained that he still didn't want a wife or family. And she still did.

They could remain lovers for an unspecified amount of time, enjoy each other's company and the magic they created together between the sheets. But it wouldn't last, and she had to decide whether to delude herself for a couple months, then deal with the pain of his eventual rejection, or take the handful of blissful memories they'd created already and cut her losses.

Peter returned then, breaking into her thoughts as the mattress bowed beneath his weight. She rolled into his bare thigh, finally forcing her eyes open to stare up at him.

"You look like a Greek goddess, replete after an afternoon of being pleasured by her love slaves."

The back of his hand dusted the length of her arm,

sending shivers down her spine. "Just one love slave," she corrected. "But he's very talented."

"Thanks." One corner of his mouth quirked in a sexy half-grin. "I aim to please. Speaking of which, we need more condoms if we hope to repeat the performance on the floor, or in the tub, or anywhere else. I'm going to run down to the gift shop and see what they have. Don't move, okay?"

She didn't move, but neither did she nod in agreement.

He retrieved his slacks and shirt from the pile on the floor, shrugging into them as he headed for the door. Checking for his wallet, he threw her a wink and wave from the hallway just before the door slammed shut.

Lucy lay there for a minute, letting her mind race and trying to decide what to do. Then she slowly got out of bed and began to dress in the same purple business suit she'd worn for the trip up.

Dragging her suitcase from the closet, she threw her belongings inside in no particular order, her movements becoming more and more hurried the longer she took, afraid Peter would return before she'd completed her task.

If he caught her trying to sneak out, there's no telling how he would react, and she wasn't sure she could explain. She just knew she couldn't stay here a minute longer.

She double-checked the drawers and bathroom counter, then quickly used the automatic checkout on the television set to let the hotel know she was leaving. No sense letting them charge him for nights she wasn't even using.

Peter would be crushed when he came back and found the room empty. She knew that, and yet she couldn't spend the rest of the night with him, no matter how much it might hurt his feelings not to. She couldn't finish out their trip as his lover when there was no hope of ever being more.

As she passed the door that connected their two rooms, she stopped and took a deep breath. Pressing a kiss to her fingertips, she then touched them to the cool panel.

"I'm sorry," she whispered, as though he could hear her and might someday understand her decision and the price she paid in making it.

With tears gathering along the rims of her eyes, she hurried out of the room and down the carpeted hall toward the stairwell exit.

Nine

Peter was whistling as he returned to the room and knocked on the faux wood panel. He had his key card, but it wouldn't work on her door. And as lovely as Lucy had looked when he left, stretched across the bed gloriously naked, he knew she wouldn't mind jumping up to answer his summons. After all, he came bearing gifts…the kind that would allow them to make love at least a dozen more times before morning.

The thought brought a wide smile to his face. He continued whistling and waited.

Maybe she'd fallen asleep. He rapped again and then listened for noises that would mean she was moving around inside.

Okay, so maybe she was really, *really* asleep. No problem. He'd go in through his room, crawl into bed with her, and proceed to wake her with long, wet kisses up and down the line of her bare body. The thought turned him hard and caused the blood to rush heatedly through his veins in anticipation.

Or maybe she was taking a bath. In which case, he'd strip down to his birthday suit and join her in the warm, sudsy water. This hotel had nice, roomy tubs with plenty of erotic potential.

Deciding to leave her to whatever she was doing, he took a few steps to the side and opened his own door, the gift shop bag rattling as he juggled it to get the job done. He crossed the room and went through the connecting door, noticing right away that she was no longer in bed.

She must be in the bathroom, then. He didn't hear the water running, but that only meant she wasn't taking a shower. She had probably run a bath as soon as he'd left and was even now luxuriating beneath a layer of fluffy bubbles.

He dug inside the brown paper sack and pried a single condom out of the box. *Always be prepared.* He recited the Boy Scout motto with silent amusement, clasping the protection in his tightened fist.

When he reached the bathroom, though, the door stood wide open. The lights were off and the room was empty.

Peter frowned, turning his head to search the entire

hotel room, even as he realized the effort was futile. The rooms weren't that big, and it wasn't like she'd be hiding in the closet or under the bed.

Still, just to be sure, he checked both places. Then he stalked over to his room, repeating the process. Lucy was nowhere to be found.

Maybe she'd thought of something she needed and run down to the gift shop herself right after he'd left, and they'd simply missed crossing each other's paths.

Figuring that was the most likely scenario, Peter stuffed the loose condom in his pocket and moved to the mini-bar for a drink. She'd be back any minute now, and he didn't want to be dehydrated for their next bout of mind-blowing, teeth-rattling sex.

God, but Lucy turned him on. It wasn't just her long, luxurious black hair or the red-hot come-and-get-me lipstick she normally wore. Not just her body or the way she moved it, which could tempt a saint to sin. It was so much more than that, even if he couldn't quite put it into words.

She made him feel good—aroused as hell nine times out of ten, but also happy, comfortable, safe, accepted. When she was around, he just felt…better, in every way imaginable.

He looked forward to her arrival at his house each morning and knew she'd have everything under control while she was there. But it was more than just his reliance on her as a personal assistant, more than simply her extreme competence in the workplace.

He could have hired anyone to answer the phone, deal with his correspondence, and charm his associates. Lucy was exceptionally talented at those things, he'd be the first to admit, but he doubted any other employee would plague his thoughts the way she did or make him break his own iron-clad rule about not getting seriously involved.

He was involved, all right. Dammit. And he didn't know quite what to do about it, except to go with the flow until a solution came to mind.

Slugging back the last of his bottled water, he raided the small refrigerator for something a little stronger. This time, he grabbed a gin and mixed it with a splash of tonic in one of the glasses that the hotel provided.

He was on his fourth trip back from the mini-bar, drinking scotch straight from a tiny plastic bottle, when he realized Lucy had been gone for over thirty minutes.

Where the hell was she?

The gift shop had been on the verge of closing when he was down there, so she couldn't still be shopping. He racked his brain, but couldn't think of anywhere else she might have gone, especially without leaving a note.

With a curse, Peter stood, smacking a hand to his forehead. A note. He'd checked the rooms for Lucy, but hadn't thought to look for a note. Duh!

Leaving the half-full bottle of scotch on the night-stand with his growing collection of empties, he went back to her room. The scratch pad on the bedside table was blank, as was the hotel letterhead in the desk drawer, and he didn't see a slip of paper anywhere.

The only other place he could think of where she might have left a note was the bathroom mirror or countertop.

The reflective sliding doors of the closet stood open as he passed and what he saw from the corner of his eye froze him in his tracks.

The closet was empty. He hadn't noticed before, or at least it hadn't registered in his otherwise preoccupied brain, but the closet was completely and utterly empty, except for the bare wooden hangers and plastic dry cleaning bag provided by the hotel. No suitcase, no bright, tailored business suits, no sign of Lucy's presence whatsoever.

A sinking, slimy feeling began to uncoil low in Peter's gut. Bleak, heavy footsteps carried him to the dresser, where he discovered the drawers to be as vacant as the rest of the room.

My God, she was gone. Not just off on an errand, but dressed, packed and checked out.

He sat down heavily on the end of the unmade bed, disbelief washing over him.

Why? Why would she leave when things had been going so well between them? His mind couldn't even begin to wrap itself around the concept.

Where could she have gone? To another hotel? The airport? Back to Georgetown? He wasn't even sure how to find out.

And then he had to wonder if he *wanted* to. She'd taken off just when he thought they were closer than ever, which meant his radar was seriously skewed.

What if he located her, only to have her tell him she never wanted to see him again?

A hard fist squeezed around his heart at the very thought.

He wasn't sure he could handle not having Lucy in his life. Holding her at arm's length, sure. Fantasizing about her but not being able touch her, or being allowed to make love to her and then having to stop…well, it wouldn't be fun, but he could deal with it.

But not having her around, not seeing her on a daily basis, not hearing her sexy, throaty voice and watching the sway of her hips as she walked down the hall…

No. He refused to contemplate such a thing.

Lucy's mindset was a mystery to him. He couldn't possibly know what she was thinking or what had driven her to leave him this way, but he could certainly find out and take steps to rectify the situation.

If that meant promising to put their relationship back on a strictly professional keel, so be it. It might turn him into a hollow shell of a man or send him into the arms of a dozen faceless women for some semblance of meaningless intimacy, but if it kept Lucy around and feeling secure, then he would do it. Happily, regardless of his own personal suffering.

Taking a deep breath, he got to his feet, then blew the air out through his nose. Fine. She'd sneaked out five minutes after making love with him, so it was obvious she wanted to be alone. He'd let her. He'd finish up his business here in New York with William Dawson, which should only take another day or so, then he'd head back to Georgetown and see how Lucy acted toward him. Try to feel her out about how she wanted their relationship to progress from there.

That would give them both a little time to cool down and think things over. Then maybe they could decide together what to do. Lord knew he'd bungled the situation enough on his own.

The wheels of Lucy's suitcase rolled over the toe of her shoe as she came to a stop in front of her apartment door and she swore in pain. She was tired and stiff from the sudden trip home, and on the way to being depressed about her decision to leave Peter alone at the hotel.

But it was for the best…or so she kept telling herself.

Fishing the keys out of her purse, she unlocked the door and let herself in, careful to guard the entrance in case Cocoa got it into her head to slip out. The last thing she needed was to spend the night searching the corridors of the building for her runaway cat.

She flipped on the kitchen light and was surprised to find Cocoa nowhere in sight. Usually the kitty met her at the door and couldn't wait to be scratched behind the ears or given a quick snack.

Lord, she hoped Ethan hadn't dropped the ball and let her cat either escape or starve to death.

But Cocoa's food dish sat in the middle of the table, looking freshly licked clean. And the water bowl in the corner was full.

With a frown, she started tiptoeing through the apartment, looking for signs of life. And as she rounded the corner into the living area, she had to bite down on a chuckle to keep from waking both the man and feline asleep on her couch.

Cocoa lay perched on Ethan's gently rising and falling chest while Ethan's hand rested over the calico's mottled back. An infomercial playing on the television in the background, casting blue and yellow shadows over the two forms.

Sensing her presence, Ethan slowly came awake, blinking to bring her into focus. "Hey," he almost croaked. "I didn't expect you back so soon."

"Obviously." She grinned and moved closer to give Cocoa a pat.

"Where's Peter?" he asked, glancing around as though he expected his friend to suddenly appear behind Lucy.

At the mention of Peter's name, her lips thinned. "He's still in New York," she told him, averting her gaze and taking several steps away.

Ethan sat up, careful not to jar the sleeping cat unnecessarily. Unperturbed, Cocoa jumped from Ethan's stomach to the couch cushion, then stopped to yawn and stretch before curling up and going back to her nap.

Getting to his feet, Ethan brushed the stray fur from his shirt front before turning his attention back to her. "Did something happen between the two of you?"

She lifted her head, meeting his eyes once again. His insight stunned her, but then, he was Peter's best friend, so maybe she shouldn't be surprised by how well they knew each other.

"You could say that."

He stuck a thumb into the waistband of his jeans, cocking his hip to the side. "Was it good or bad?"

"First it was good," she said, remembering their lovemaking as not just "good" but spectacular. "And then it was bad."

"I take it Peter did or said something to upset you."

Lucy sighed, rubbing the spot between her brows where a headache was forming. "Actually, he didn't. I just…"

Her throat closed with emotion and she turned away to get hold of herself. Crossing the kitchen, she pulled a container of orange juice from the fridge and poured a glass. She offered to do the same for Ethan, but he shook his head.

"I love him," she admitted, the words going down better with a sip of juice.

A beat of silence passed and then he said simply, "I know."

She glanced up at him, standing on the other side of the kitchen table, jaw slack in astonishment.

"Come on, Lucy, I've seen the two of you together.

I didn't notice anything at first, but lately… Lately, it's become more obvious," he finished.

A flush of heat crept over her features as she realized she hadn't hidden her feelings for Peter all this time as well as she'd thought.

"Don't worry," he told her, practically reading her mind. "I don't think anyone else has noticed, least of all Peter the Oblivious."

Wetting her lips, she turned and made a production of putting her empty glass in the sink and returning the orange juice to the refrigerator. "So the fact that he feels nothing for me is also…obvious."

"I don't know about that."

Ethan came up behind her, placing his hands on her shoulders and giving them a light squeeze.

"Like I said, Peter tends to be oblivious. I think he feels plenty for you, he just won't admit it, even to himself."

She didn't know how to respond to that or where to begin with the questions clamoring in her brain.

"You could still go out with me," he suggested, blowing in her ear. "I've been asking you out for months. So maybe now you'll cut Peter loose and give me a shot."

She spun around, spearing him with an annoyed glance. "You would do that? To your best friend?"

"For a pretty woman?" He gave a snort. "Hell, yes."

"Let me clear this up for you once and for all," she snapped, physically removing his hands from where they rested on her upper arms. "Not on your life. Not even if you were the last man on earth. *Especially* if you were the last man on earth because I would never want to take the chance of letting you breed and spread your reprehensible DNA on to another human being."

Stalking across the tiled kitchen, she put her hand on the doorknob before turning back to him with a scowl on her face. "I think you should leave."

Ethan held his hands up in surrender. "Whoa, there, take it easy. I was testing you." He moved back to the table, straddling one of the spindle-back chairs as he held her gaze. "You gave exactly the right answer, by the way. And I may talk tough, but for your information, I *wouldn't* move in on a friend's girl. At least not one he's genuinely interested in."

Some of the fire went out of her at his admission and she dragged herself over to take the chair opposite him, feeling even more tired and weary than when she'd arrived.

"You say that like you believe it. I just wish I could."

"I don't think Peter does, either. Or he's afraid to. And going out with me would be one sure way of finding out…either he'd let it go and you'd know for certain he had no feelings for you, or he'd go through the roof and you'd know he does."

He gave her a hopeful look, which Lucy now recognized as simply teasing.

"There is one other option," he offered. "Come to work for me at The Hot Spot."

She raised a brow at the unexpected proposal.

"I know I've tried to lure you away from Peter before—only partly in jest, since I'm jealous as hell that he gets such a great assistant and I'm stuck running my business myself. But maybe now is the time to make a change. Get away from him for a while. Give him some time and space to think about what he's lost and how he really feels about you. You can always go back later; you know I won't hold you to anything, and Peter would be stupid not to give you your old job back if you wanted it."

"Do you really think I should?"

"I do. Peter and I have been friends for a lot of years. I know how his mind works and how hard it's going to be for you to face him while things are still up in the air between you. Consider my club part-time work while you figure things out."

The minutes ticked by while she considered his offer from every angle. In the end, though, it came down to only a single point: she didn't think she could bear to see Peter bright and early Monday morning with her heart still raw and bleeding, so soon after leaving him alone in that hotel room.

Taking a deep breath, she looked at Ethan—her new boss, if only for a while—and nodded.

Ten

Well, those had been two of the longest, most excruciating days of his life.

Normally he loved delving into a computer system, finding all its bugs and quirks, and then putting it back together to run even more efficiently. But this time, every moment had felt like an eternity. Every word Will Dawson had uttered, every joke he'd tried to crack to lighten Peter's mood had grated on his nerves.

He'd done the bare minimum to improve Dawson's productivity and then promised to return at a later date to smooth out the edges so he could jump on a plane and head back to Georgetown.

It was two in the afternoon by the time he arrived,

but that was okay because it meant Lucy would be at his house, working, and he would get the chance to talk things through with her instead of waiting another day to hash out their differences.

When he reached his town house, he used his key to unlock the front door and dropped his overnight bag just inside on the foyer floor. Cocking his head, he listened for the telltale sounds of Lucy's fingers at the keyboard of her computer or the soft classical music radio station she sometimes turned on while she worked.

He didn't hear anything, but that didn't mean she wasn't there.

A thread of doubt niggled as he closed the door and noticed the pile of mail spread across the carpet. Strange that Lucy hadn't gathered it up already. She usually did, first thing. But maybe she'd forgotten or gotten busy doing something else.

Yeah, a tiny voice in his head replied sarcastically, *forgot to pick up the mail when she'd done it automatically every day for the past two years.*

But he wasn't giving up yet. Moving through the house, he checked the study that doubled as her office and pretended not to notice that her computer was turned off and the call light on the telephone was blinking uncontrollably.

So she hadn't had a chance to boot up or collect messages yet. That didn't mean anything. There were plenty of days when she went to the kitchen to start a pot of coffee or up to his office to clean up a bit before getting started.

From there, he peeked his head into the den, the kitchen, then climbed the stairs for a quick sweep of his own office and bedroom. Not that he expected to find her in either place.

His heart sank and his mouth grew dry as he realized she wasn't there. From the mail on the hall floor and the number of calls stored up on the phone, it didn't look like she'd been to work at all since returning from New York.

The knowledge worried Peter more than a little, but he tried not to panic. She was probably still upset by whatever had driven her to run out on him after they'd made love and just needed a day or two more to get herself together enough to face him.

Or maybe she was waiting for him to contact her and say he was sorry. He was as clueless about what he needed to apologize for as he was about why she'd abandoned him in Manhattan in the first place, but if there was one thing he knew for sure about women, it was that the man was always wrong, the woman was always right, and it was the man's place to say he was sorry before things got too far out of hand.

That, he could do. Because a part of him was sorry…for whatever had spurred her to take off on him. For not having the self-control to keep from making love to her the first time *and* the second, when he knew nothing could come of it. And for not being the man she wanted him to be, one who could provide her with the future she so desperately needed.

Scrubbing a hand over his face, he ran back downstairs for his luggage, and decided to put the new mail on her desk along the way.

As long as he was there, he might as well check the waiting messages, too. With any luck, Lucy might have called and he would have an idea of what was on her mind. If not, he'd have helped her out a bit and not left quite so much for her to catch up on once she finally returned to work.

He sat down at her desk and grabbed a notepad and pen, then punched the buttons necessary to access voicemail. Business call, business call, phone company calling about Lucy's request to add another line to the house, business call… He wrote everything down, thinking he could probably take care of a few of these on his own, but would leave the important ones for Lucy.

Then her voice drifted out to him through the speakerphone and a hitch of awareness rolled over him, sending his pulse rate stuttering. She sounded stiff and unhappy, but he chalked that up to the mechanics of the electronic technology.

And then her words began to sink in. She hadn't phoned to explain why she'd left New York without him or to ask for a couple days off while she got her thoughts and feelings in order. She was blowing him off.

Peter, this is Lucy. I'm just calling to let you know

that I've accepted another position and won't be back to work. I'll be by within the next couple of weeks to collect my things, unless you'd rather send them to me. I'm sorry I couldn't give you more notice, but my new job begins immediately. I'm sure you'll find someone to take my place in no time.

He sat, stunned, for several long minutes while the rest of the messages played through unheard. Her words echoed over and over again in his ears, making him feel light-headed and more confused than ever.

Why? Why would she take another job? Nothing that had happened between them was so awful that she needed to *quit*.

And *take her place?*

How was he ever supposed to find someone to replace her? Someone competent, reliable, and willing enough to do all the things he needed taken care of on a daily basis. It had been miraculous enough to find Lucy to begin with, he couldn't even begin to be lucky enough to find a second decent assistant.

But was that really the part that was bothering him so much? The fact that he was losing his favorite secretary?

Hell, no. He was on the verge of a breakdown because this was *Lucy* and she'd just left him. Left his employ, left his house, left *him*.

He wasn't going to get the chance to find out why she'd sneaked out while he was off buying condoms.

He wouldn't be able to apologize for whatever had upset her and promise to make things right.

It seemed Lucy wasn't interested in repairing their relationship—not even their professional one.

The hollow sensation at the base of his gut began to fill…but not with acceptance, with anger.

She didn't want anything more to do with him? Fine. He didn't want anything more to do with her, either.

His feelings for her had been nothing more than lust, anyway. And maybe a fraction of dependence, for the way she took such good care of everything for him.

But all that was over now. She'd quit, taken another job. From now on, she wouldn't be around for him to fantasize about or desire or rely on.

A part of him wanted to mourn that fact, but then the logical side of his brain kicked in and reminded him that this was probably all for the best. Just because they'd spent a few very memorable moments in each other's company didn't mean they had a future together. He'd known that all along and had never wanted Lucy to be hurt. So maybe having her leave now was better than having to push her away later.

It sounded good, and in a few days, Peter thought he might even start to believe it.

"Set 'em up again."

"Are you sure?" Ethan asked. "You've already had quite a bit."

Peter scowled at his so-called friend and tapped the

bar in front of him where three empty shot glasses and three empty beer bottles sat. "Don't lecture me on the evils of alcohol, just keep them coming."

Ethan held his tongue, pouring another finger of whiskey with a beer chaser, just as Peter had ordered when he'd first walked into The Hot Spot.

At this time of day, the club was officially closed, but Ethan and some of the other staff came in early to set up and check supplies for the evening crush. A Top Forty ballad played softly in the background, but by eight o'clock tonight, the speakers would be blaring with rock, disco, rap…whatever the party crowd liked best.

The idea of people drinking, dancing, having fun made Peter scowl even harder. He was miserable and the rest of the world should be, too, dammit!

"So…" Ethan ventured while Peter nursed his beer, "are you going to tell me what's bothering you, or do I have to wait until you drink me out of all my profits?"

He thought about making a smart remark, telling Ethan to mind his own business, but he'd come here with the sole intention of getting a little advice from his best friend. Or at the very least, spilling his guts and hoping the sour taste in his mouth would finally go away.

"Lucy," he said simply, noticing the way her name caught in his throat. He had to swallow hard before he could even take another sip of his beer.

"What about her?" his friend asked, filling a segmented tray with bits of fruit and olives for mixed drinks.

"She left me."

"For another job, you mean?"

A beat passed before he answered. "Yeah." Among other things. "She quit and went to work for somebody else."

"Lucky bastard. She's a real treasure, that one. So what did you do to run her off?"

At that, Peter's brows lifted, then turned down in annoyance. "What makes you think I ran her off?"

"For one thing, you slept with her. And I know you, buddy. You're not big on commitment. The women you date and take to bed may all look different—tall, short; stacked, petite; blonde, brunette, redhead—but they have one thing in common: they're easy to pry yourself away from. You don't promise them anything more than a couple of good rolls in the hay and maybe a photo op or two when you take them along to social events, and they don't expect it."

"What's your point?" Peter asked, wondering why he stayed friends with this guy when he was turning into such a colossal pain in the ass.

"My point, Mr. Grumpy Pants, is that Lucy isn't like those other women, and you damn well know it. You knew it before the two of you ever got stuck in that elevator together. She's not the kind of girl you can just have sex with and then not call in the morning. The kind who's good for a thrill, but who won't expect more.

Lucy isn't clingy or demanding, but she's also not looking for a fling."

With a huff of frustration, Ethan slammed down a jar of maraschino cherries, then braced his hands on the edge of the bar. "Holy heck, Peter, when did you get so damn dense? She's in love with you, for God's sake. Probably has been since the day she started working for you."

Peter felt as though his friend had just dropped a ton of bricks on his head. He couldn't have been more stunned if Lucy had materialized at that very moment in a G-string and pasties and started dancing on the countertop for dollar bills.

"What are you talking about? Lucy doesn't have those sorts of feelings for me. She's a great gal, don't get me wrong, but her problem with our sleeping together wasn't that she was in love with me, it's that I was also her boss. The conflict of interest made her uncomfortable."

Ethan rolled his eyes and muttered some truly creative curses beneath his breath. "'Great gal,'" he repeated. "'Conflict of interest.' Man, I'm surprised you can dress yourself in the morning. Did all that booze I served you kill off your last functioning brain cells?"

He leaned across the bar, so close Peter's eyes nearly crossed trying to keep him in focus.

"Haven't you ever noticed the way she looks at you? Or the way she cleans your house and takes care of you?"

His head ached and his memory was becoming suddenly fuzzy. "She doesn't look at me any differently than she does anyone else. And as for cleaning up…that's part of her job."

"Blind as well as dumb," Ethan mumbled with a toss of his head. "She looks at you like the stars in the night sky were your idea, Peter. She's certainly never looked at me that way. She also thinks you're the smartest, most talented man ever to design a computer game. Now, granted, you're good at what you do, but to hear Lucy tell it, you might as well be Bill Gates, Mahatma Gandhi, and the president of the United States all rolled into one.

Ethan pulled the towel from his shoulder and wiped cherry juice off the bar. "And she cleans up after you and makes sure you have everything you need or want because she *cares* about you, not because she thinks she's being a good little assistant. She's *in love* with you, you big blockhead."

Peter's chest tightened. His heart was pounding a thousand beats per second and his lungs refused to draw in oxygen. Ethan was wrong. He had to be.

Peter had met women like that before, diamond rings dancing in their eyes. He identified the look immediately and always managed to keep them at bay.

If Lucy had harbored feelings for him all this time, he would have noticed. His force fields would have gone up, and he damn sure wouldn't have let himself get involved with her, no matter how badly he might have wanted to sample her luscious body.

"No," he said, shaking his head in acute denial. "No, I think you're wrong."

He knew Lucy wanted the big picture from whatever man she eventually ended up with, but he hadn't gone so far as to assume *love* was involved.

"Oh, yeah?" Ethan seemed amused now. He pushed away from the bar and leaned back against the low shelf of colorful liquor bottles. "Maybe this will get through to you, then. I'm Lucy's new boss. She came home from New York alone and upset, and I offered her a job here because she said she couldn't stand the thought of working with you every day for the rest of her life. She's upstairs right now, in the office."

"What?" Peter leapt to his feet, the bar stool teetering at the speed with which he left it.

Ethan took a menacing step forward. "Don't even think about it," he warned in a low voice. "She doesn't want to see you, and I promised her I wouldn't tell you she was here, so if you move so much as an inch in that direction, I'll have to ask Archie to take you out back and pummel you a while."

Archie was Ethan's head bouncer, built like an eighteen-wheeler, and Peter searched for a glimpse of him as he turned his attention to the glass-fronted office on the second floor of the nightclub. He didn't see any signs of Lucy because the blinds were drawn, but the urge to climb the curved staircase at the back of the room and find her was strong.

Ethan came out from behind the bar and laid a hand

on Peter's shoulder. "You've screwed this up royally, buddy, and I'm not real sure it can be fixed. But before you do anything, you need to go home and sleep off your little drinking binge. I already called a cab. When you wake up, take a long, hard look at this thing and how you feel about Lucy, then maybe you can talk to her."

Feeling like he was walking through a thick fog, Peter nodded. His friend's words didn't make complete sense at this very moment, but he knew Ethan was looking out for his best interests. Even if he had hired Lucy behind his back, he wouldn't give Peter bad advice. They'd been friends too long for that.

With a nod, he let Ethan lead him outside and put him in a bright yellow taxi.

"Get some rest," Ethan told him in an understanding tone. "We'll talk later, and I'll take good care of Lucy until you decide what you're going to do."

Even as exhaustion swept him and his eyes fell closed, Peter realized that's exactly what he was afraid of—someone else taking care of Lucy because he was too screwed up to do it himself.

Lucy peered through a slit in the vertical window blinds of Ethan's office, careful not to let Peter see her. She suspected Ethan had already told him she was up here, otherwise he wouldn't have been staring so intently in her direction. But he didn't start forward, didn't storm up the stairs to confront her about quitting her job with so little advance warning. If he had, she'd have probably gone running, escaping through the emergency fire exit at her back.

Instead, Ethan laid an arm across Peter's shoulders and steered him toward the entrance of the club, presumably to send him home. She hoped Ethan had called him a cab, considering the amount of alcohol Peter had consumed since arriving only a few short hours ago.

A frown marred her brow as she considered that. Peter wasn't a big drinker. He might have a glass of wine with dinner or the occasional scotch and soda at the end of the day, but other than that, his main vice seemed to be gallons upon gallons of sugary-sweet cola. Today, she hadn't seen him order so much as a ginger ale.

That bothered her, probably more than it should have. She didn't work for Peter any longer, which meant his eating and drinking habits were none of her concern.

But she still loved him, despite her best efforts to lock him out of her heart, so she supposed it was only natural to wonder about him and worry that he wasn't taking good enough care of himself.

Ethan came back inside alone and headed directly for the polished onyx stairs that led to his office. Lucy let the blinds fall from her hands and darted back to the desk, managing to take a seat and look busy just as the door opened.

She glanced up and smiled, pretending she'd been working on his books all along. "Hi."

He didn't return her greeting. "Peter just left," he reported flatly.

Her eyes widened as she feigned a sense of startlement. "He was here?"

One corner of his mouth curved in mock amusement. "Peter may have been too drunk to notice you peeking through the blinds, but I sure wasn't." He shook his head. "You two are really something. Both so desperate to pretend you don't feel anything for the other that you're sort of missing the point."

Lucy bristled slightly at his chastising tone. He'd been so supportive up until now, she'd hate for him to suddenly turn critical of her feelings for his friend. "What point would that be?"

"That you love each other. You should be together, celebrating that love, not working this hard to come up with ways to hide it."

"And you're such an expert on the subject?" She made it a question because she knew all about Ethan's reputation as a ladies' man and his track record with women.

"No. That's just it. I haven't had much luck in the romance department myself, but it's always easier to see the truth of a situation when you're not personally involved. And it's pretty darn clear from where I'm standing that you and Peter feel the same about each other, you're just too damn stubborn to admit it or take a chance on being shot down."

Her eyes welled with sudden tears at Ethan's words. Was he right? Was she being a coward? If she walked up to Peter and told him exactly how she felt, would he surprise her by admitting he loved her, too?

Her gut told her no, that he would stick to his long-held beliefs that he couldn't open himself to a relationship and still be a successful entrepreneur. But a tiny voice in her head asked *what if?*

What if she was wrong?

What if he did feel something for her?

What if she held her tongue out of fear when all it would take was one well-placed question to possibly make all her dreams come true?

But was she brave enough to risk it? She didn't know. Ethan had given her something to think about, though, and she promised herself that she would.

Blinking to disperse the dampness fringing her lashes, she inclined her head to let him know she heard what he was saying.

"Do you know why Peter won't let himself get involved?" she asked, wondering if they were close enough for Peter to have shared his past with his friend.

"Yeah, I know," Ethan said with a derisive curl of his lip. "And if you ask me, he doesn't give himself enough credit. But I have a feeling that when he finally stops worrying about turning into his father, he'll discover he's not half bad at juggling his software company and a family."

Lucy swallowed hard, trying to dislodge the lump in her throat. "I've always thought the same thing."

"So tell him," Ethan said simply. "And then make him believe it."

Eleven

Three days. Three days without Lucy and he had yet to sleep, eat, or change his clothes. He hadn't showered or shaved, and had barely touched the case of soda she always made sure to keep in the refrigerator for him.

As soon as he'd gotten home from The Hot Spot; instead of taking Ethan's advice and sleeping it off, he'd stripped down to his boxers and undershirt and gone straight to work on a new computer program.

He'd worked for hours, days, but nothing seemed to go the way it was supposed to. Ideas were slower to come, codes harder to write, and solutions more difficult to find. His mind kept wandering—always to Lucy and how much he missed her. To what might have been.

Without her here, his house was a just a big, empty building, with cold walls and even colder rooms. The entire place was dark because she wasn't around to flip on the lights.

The phone rang, but he didn't pick up. There was no one in the world he wanted to talk to right now except Lucy, and he doubted she would be calling anytime soon.

Ethan had told him he needed to think things over, decide what he really wanted. Since then, all he'd done was *think,* but he still didn't know what to do.

He knew what he wanted, but only in general terms: Lucy. He wanted her to come back to work, be in his life—and his bed—again. But he was smart enough to realize that as far as going back to the way things were, that ship had sailed. He couldn't go to her and say, *Hey, how about being my lover and my assistant again, but without all that pesky emotional baggage?* He suspected that would go over about as well as a Yankee fan at a Red Sox home game.

And to be honest, he wasn't positive that's what he wanted any longer, either. He still didn't think it was a good idea to mix business with pleasure.

His father had been an abysmal failure when he'd tried to handle the jobs of both father and businessman, but Peter was beginning to wonder if trying and possibly failing in the long run still wasn't a better alternative than never trying at all. Especially if it meant the difference between having Lucy in his life or not having Lucy in his life.

Because *not* having her was becoming unbearable.

He pictured his life ten years from now, without Lucy being a part of it, and all he saw was darkness, sadness, misery.

Oh, he might be sinfully rich and famous for his games and software designs, but most likely he would also be a lonely hermit.

His assistants would be pimply-faced college interns from the local university who didn't stick around long enough for him to learn their names.

Women would flirt with him at social events or drop by with baked goods to try to lure him out, but none of them would be as attractive or interesting as Lucy. And he already knew with complete conviction that no other woman would ever touch him the way she had, emotionally or physically.

So what are you going to do about it, smart guy? a voice in his head whispered none too subtly.

Good question. He didn't have an answer just yet, but since it didn't look like he'd be going to bed anytime soon, he certainly had time to figure it out.

Lucy stood on the stoop outside Peter's front door, breathing deeply, concentrating on not hyperventilating. She didn't want to be here, had half hoped he would ship the last of her things so she would never have to see him again.

No, that wasn't quite true. She wished on a daily

basis that she could see him…not to mention touch him, smell him, hear his low, rumbling voice.

God, she missed him, and they hadn't even been apart a week yet.

Her stomach took a tumble and she locked her teeth together to keep from throwing up. Lord, she was nervous. She'd come to collect her things, but only if Plan A didn't work out.

Ethan's way was Plan A because she hadn't been able to get his comments out of her head since he'd told her to go down fighting, instead of feeling sorry for herself and giving up like she had when she'd flown home from New York.

So here she was, preparing to confront Peter and lay all her cards out on the table, regardless of how he might react. Her heart would shatter like glass if he rejected her or told her again that he couldn't get seriously involved because it might influence his work. But she was willing to risk it on the off chance that Ethan was right. Even if the odds were a zillion to one, she had to know for sure.

Swallowing the knot of dread lodged in her throat, she lifted her hand and rang the doorbell. She still had a key, but didn't feel right using it when she no longer worked for him.

She waited for Peter to answer the door and braced herself for the sight of him, but he never came. Seconds ticked by and she pressed the bell again.

This time, she heard the thump of footsteps on the staircase and mumbled curses. The door swung open before she was fully prepared, stealing the air from her lungs.

Peter stood on the other side of the threshold, fully dressed in a light blue suit and pale yellow tie. His shoes were polished to a high shine, his hair neatly combed. It was enough to stun her into speechlessness.

"Lucy."

Her name burst from his lips in a rush, breathless from more than just the race downstairs, she suspected.

"Peter. I, um…came for my things."

Coward! she chastised herself. *Wimp. You weren't going to say that.*

But he took a step back, motioning her inside. "Come in. I'm glad to see you," he said as he closed the door behind them. "I was actually planning to come by The Hot Spot soon to talk to you. I guess you've saved me the trouble."

She gave a weak smile, not sure how to respond to that. She suppose she should be grateful she'd decided to come over, somewhat prepared, before he could catch her off guard at the club.

At the look on her face, he stumbled. "Jeez, I didn't mean it that way. Going to see you wouldn't have been an inconvenience at all. I just meant…we must be on the same wavelength for you to show up here at about the same time I was getting ready to come see you."

Her grin grew a little then, becoming more sincere as he rushed to correct himself and reassure her. This was the Peter she knew, always aware and courteous of her feelings. The suit had thrown her off at first, but the hair, the eyes, the lips, the shape of his well-shaven, chiseled face were all familiar and dear to her heart.

She curled her fingers into her palm, resisting the urge to reach up and smooth a stray lock away from his forehead.

"Your things are all where you left them," he said, walking backwards ahead of her as he gestured toward the den. A slight blush tinged his cheeks. "I was sort of hoping you'd come back to work so I wouldn't have to gather them up at all."

She held his gaze for a split second, then looked away, studying the oriental design on the red and beige runner that covered the hardwood floor.

"Actually," she ventured, steeling her spine and forcing her chin up, "I didn't come only to collect my belongings. I also wanted to talk. About us."

She saw his chest hitch as he sucked in a breath, and her hopes flagged. Oh, God, this wasn't going well at all. He hadn't changed his mind. He didn't want her back—at least not as anything more than his assistant. Her pulse pounded in her ears and she wanted to turn and run, except her feet wouldn't seem to move.

And then Peter reached out and wrapped his warm, strong fingers around her wrist, sending a shock of electricity skittering along her nerve endings.

"Wait here," he told her. "I'll be right back."

Part of her wondered why she was just standing

there, rooted to the spot. She should leave, or at least begin clearing her desk.

· But Peter bounded up the stairs, returning less than a minute later carrying his brown leather briefcase. He grabbed her hand on the way past and dragged her into the study.

"Sit," he ordered, taking the chair beside her desk and setting the briefcase down on top to open.

Lucy bristled slightly at his perfunctory tone and she locked her knees rather than doing as he'd instructed.

"I don't need to sit," she said, finding a bit of her courage in the annoyance he'd stirred up. Funny how she could still love him and be ready to spill her guts about it even after he'd rubbed her the wrong way. "But there is something I need to say to you."

He raised his head, green eyes washing over her like a cool breeze over a meadow. A muscle ticked in his jaw. "I need to say something to you, too," he said softly, though his voice was strained.

He probably wanted to beg her to come back to work, but she couldn't do that, given the way things stood at the moment.

"Please," she murmured. "Let me go first." She had to get this out before she exploded, and hearing Peter ask her to resume her position as his assistant would only weaken her resolve.

The sinews of his neck contracted and released as he swallowed, but he inclined his head for her to continue. Inhaling deeply, she tried to get her thoughts in order and figure out where to begin. She took a seat, finally, before her legs gave out and she ended up on the floor.

"I'm sorry about running off that night at the hotel," she admitted. "I didn't mean to worry or upset you, but I just couldn't handle what was happening between us and had to get out of there."

She laid her hand atop his where it rested on the edge of the briefcase. The heat from his skin soaked through to her bones, comforting her more than she'd expected.

"The fact is, Peter, I have feelings for you. You've probably figured that out already," she added with a touch of a smile, "but what you don't know is that I've felt this way for the past two years, ever since I started working for you."

Panic raced through Peter's veins, causing his eyes to go wide and fear to clog his windpipe. "Wait, wait, wait!" he all but shouted. "Don't say anything else."

He leapt to his feet, shaking his head and digging frantically through the papers in his briefcase. She was about to say she loved him, he could sense it. And while he wanted to hear those three little words from her mouth almost more than he wanted to draw his next breath, *he* needed to be the one to say them first. He'd fought this for so long, put her through so much, he wanted her to know how he felt about her before she said any more.

Finding what he was searching for, he dropped back onto the seat of his chair and turned to face Lucy once again. She looked startled and confused by his sudden outburst, and he didn't blame her one bit.

Pulling his chair a few inches closer, he braced his knees on either side of her closed legs, lifting her hands from her lap and cradling them in his own. The paper rattled in his tight hold, but he ignored it.

"I'm the one who should be apologizing to you, Lucy," he said solemnly. "You're so good to me…you always have been. And as hard as it may be for you to believe, you've meant more to me from the very beginning, too. You're a great assistant, and I'd do just about anything to have you back on the payroll, but there's something I want from you even more than your exceptional secretarial skills."

He brushed long strands of ebony hair over her shoulder, caressing her cool cheek with his fingertips on the return trip. "I want you to be with me, Lucy. Stay with me, live with me, marry me…love me."

A flood of emotions flashed across her face, not the least of which were incredulity and wariness. Fear squeezed him low in the solar plexus. He'd known this wouldn't be easy, known she would doubt him after all his talk about never tying himself to a wife and family, never letting his personal life interfere with his business plans.

"Hear me out. Please," he said, his hand clutching hers even more tightly. "When I got back to the hotel room and found you gone, I didn't know what to do or think or feel. I'd gotten it into my head that everything was great. We could be lovers without strings, have a good time together without it ever meaning anything more. But when I realized you'd left and weren't coming back, I was faced with the fact that you *needed* more."

He lowered his gaze for a brief second, still somewhat unsure of the narrow path he was traversing. "It was one of those life-altering moments," he admitted. "I knew I had to make some serious decisions or risk losing you forever. I don't want to lose you, Luce. I love you."

The admission passed his lips quickly, and then he realized they hadn't been as difficult or as painful to utter as he'd anticipated.

"I love you," he said again, louder this time, with more conviction, even as he watched her mouth turn down with skepticism.

"I know that has to be hard for you to believe, given everything I've said in the past, but I swear on my life and the future of Reyware that it's the absolute truth. You're a part of me, Lucy, permeating every cell of my being.

"I love your hair and your eyes and the full swell of your bottom lip. I love the way you laugh and smile and take such good care of me. I love that you know what I'm thinking almost before I know myself and are as familiar with the inner workings of Reyware and Games of PRey as I am."

Licking his dry lips, he went on, willing her to trust him. "You're my inspiration, Lucy. When I got home from New York, I told myself you had been just a fling, that I could always find another assistant and certainly other lovers, and I tried to get back to work."

He chuckled shortly. "I might as well have been building a space shuttle in my basement. I couldn't think, couldn't concentrate, couldn't remember codes I'd learned as a teenager. Without you here, in my life, I'm helpless. Hopeless."

She opened her mouth to speak, but he stopped her with an index finger pressed to her lips. He was afraid she would shoot him down before he'd told her everything he needed her to hear.

"No, don't say anything. Not yet. I know I'm making it sound like I want you back just so I can work again, but that's not true. Don't you see? *You're* what makes my world go 'round. You're the one person who makes me want to get out of bed each morning to face the day…to see you and be with you. But actions speak louder than words, so I have a proposition for you."

Peter sat up straighter, smoothing the paper he'd been clutching and shoving it into her hands.

Lucy's fingers closed around the page automatically, but her head was swimming, her eyesight blurry with unshed tears. She wanted so badly for Peter to mean what he was saying, wanted so badly to believe he actually loved her even a fraction as much as she loved him. But he'd been so determined to distance himself, keep himself separate from any woman who might require a commitment, that she was afraid he was only saying what he thought she wanted to hear.

"I want you to come back to work for me," he continued before she could begin to make sense of things. "Whatever Ethan is paying you, I'll double it. Whatever perks he's giving you, I'll beat them. And this…" He tapped the paper she was holding. "I'm making you a full partner in the company. We'll share everything, fifty-fifty—the designs, the profits, the decision-making process, everything. There's only one catch."

His voice dropped to a near hush and he pushed his chair back, falling to one knee in front of her. His palm cupped the curve of her knee while the other covered the hand that held the business agreement. His gaze locked with hers, the sincerity in his dark eyes turning her resolve to mush, even as her vision swam and she had trouble making out the details of his beautiful face.

"Marry me, Lucy. Put me out of this misery of being without you. Give me a chance to show you that I can be a good husband and father and still keep my company above water."

His lips tipped up with wry humor. "I know I said it couldn't be done, but I'm willing to give it a shot. And even if I fail, even if Reyware goes under and we end up living in a cardboard box down by the river, I'd rather be in that cardboard box with you than in the most lavish mansion in the world without you."

She swallowed hard, struggling to regain her voice as her heart pounded furiously enough to burst from her chest. Twin streaks of dampness trailed down her cheeks and she blinked several times to bring Peter back into focus.

"I don't care about the money or the company. I never did," she told him quietly, tracing smooth line of his jaw and running her thumb around the alluring shape of his mouth.

"I didn't come here today just to collect my things, either. I came because Ethan warned me that if I didn't lay myself on the line and let you know how much I love you, and give you the chance to share your feelings in return, that I'd regret it for the rest of my life.

"But you do love me," she whispered, still awed by his confession and the depth of her own reciprocal feelings. "And I love you, too. So much. But, Peter, are you sure? You were so dead-set against all of this…are you sure you're really ready to get married and start a family?"

"I am totally ready," he swore with conviction. "I want to be with you for the rest of my life, Lucy Grainger. I want to watch you walk down the aisle and slip a ring on your finger that marks you as mine for all time. I want to have babies with you. I'm especially looking forward to the 'making babies' part," he said with a Groucho-like wiggle of his arched brows that made her laugh.

"I want to do my very best to be the father I never had, to be the best damn father this country has ever seen. But I'll admit, I may need your help. I need you to keep me on track, Lucy. Tell me when I'm working too hard or missing out on precious time with you or our kids. Smack me around, if you need to, but know that you come first and I really do want to make this work."

She leaned closer, until their noses almost touched. "Then we will," she told him. "We'll make it work."

And then she ran her fingers through his hair, messing up the neat style he'd probably struggled half the morning to achieve. "Just think. If I hadn't come here today, I might never have known you felt this way."

"Oh, you'd have known. Ethan told me pretty much the same thing he told you—that I needed to figure out what I wanted before it was too late. And once I knew, I'd have tracked you down to the ends of the earth to tell you what you mean to me."

Fresh tears flooded her eyes again as his words seeped through her, filling every nook and cranny of her spirit with pure contentment.

"Thank God for Ethan," she confided. "Your friend is a very smart man."

"Tell me about it," Peter said on a heartfelt sigh, drawing her down to the floor with him and into his arms. "Because *his* friend hasn't been acting very bright lately."

"Oh, I don't know." She toyed with the fringe of hair at the nape of his neck, pressing a firm kiss to his warm lips. "It seems like you came to your senses in time."

"Just in the nick of time. I don't know what I'd have

done if my stubbornness and stupidity had caused me to lose you."

"You'll never need to find out," she promised. "Now that I've got you, I'm not letting you go."

"Does that mean you'll marry me? You never did answer me before."

"Of course I will. It's all I've ever wanted."

A grin as wide as the Potomac split his face. "Me, too, although it took me a while longer to figure it out. Good thing you're a patient woman."

"Very patient."

He was loath to let go of her, now that he had her wrapped safely in the circle of his arms again, but there was one last thing he needed to do. Pulling back a little, he reached into the pocket of his suit jacket and removed a small, black velvet box. "This is for you."

He tipped open the lid and held it out to her, absorbing the look of startlement and happiness that filled her eyes as she took in the huge, marquis-cut diamond and fancy gold setting. Once he'd realized how much he loved her and decided to propose, he'd gone all out, buying the biggest, shiniest, most expensive engagement ring he thought she would accept without a fuss.

"Oh, my lord," she breathed. "It's beautiful."

Taking the ring from its satin bed, he set the box aside and slipped the band on her finger. She admired it for several moments, turning her hand this way and that so the diamond could catch the light from the window at her back. And then she turned that blazingly joyful expression on him, zapping him right down to his toes.

"What do you think?" she asked. "Should we go show Ethan and let him know his advice worked?"

Curling his hands around her waist, he waggled his brows and nuzzled the sensitive flesh just beneath her ear. "Actually, I thought maybe we could go upstairs and celebrate, make up for lost time."

"Mmm, that sounds like fun, too." Her blue eyes flashed with amusement as her arms slipped up to wind around his neck. "But afterward, we really should thank Ethan and let him know I won't be coming in to work anymore."

"We will." Peter scooped Lucy into his arms and got to his feet, heading for the stairs. "And I want to ask him to be my best man at the wedding."

"That's nice," she said, her fingers already loosening the buttons at the front of his starched white shirt. "He's your best friend, after all, and he did play the part of an unlikely matchmaker there toward the end, didn't he?"

"Yeah," he answered, taking the stairs two at a time. "But we have the blackout to thank for our start."

Epilogue

Peter scrubbed a hand over his dry, tired eyes as the last of his latest program processed across the computer screen. Stifling a yawn, he turned just as his wife tip-toed into the room.

God, he loved that word: *wife*. But he loved her even more.

She wore the same long, sapphire blue satin negligee as when they'd gone to bed several hours ago. Of course, he'd systematically stripped the gown from her body so he could make soft, sweet love to her for about an hour and a half. She must have put it back on some-time after he'd slipped away to his office.

He still worked best in the wee hours of the night,

but Lucy didn't seem to mind a bit. She simply drifted over when she thought he'd been gone too long or started to miss him, and lured him back to the bedroom.

Now, she crossed the carpeted floor in her bare feet and came to stand behind his chair, running her hands over his shoulders and across the worn cotton T-shirt covering his chest.

"How's it coming along?" she asked, her voice raspy with sleep.

He caught her fingers and folded them inside his own, holding them close above his heart. "All done. I'm just waiting for these sequences to run before I shut down."

"Think this one will be as popular as Soldiers of Misfortune?"

"It's hard to tell, but I hope so."

She sighed, resting her face against his temple where her warm breath stirred through his hair. "I'll bet it will. And then I can say 'I told you so' because you managed to design a brand new game and still be a wonderful husband, all at the same time. Amazing."

He grinned at her teasing tone and tipped his head back to meet her loving gaze. "Hey, when you're right, you're right. And this happens to be one of the few times I'm pleased to admit I was wrong, wrong, wrong."

"Me, too," she said softly, punctuating the response with a kiss.

And then she straightened, pulling him to his feet as

she tapped a few keys on his keyboard to turn off the system. Walking backward, she tugged him in the direction of their bedroom.

"I'm also pleased you have this penchant for being up at all hours. It will make things much easier on me down the road."

His brows knit in confusion at her cryptic statement and the sly smile curving her lips. "What are you talking about?"

"You know. Midnight feedings and 2:00 a.m. diaper changes. I'll leave those to you so I can sleep through the night."

He blinked, his bare feet dragging along the carpet. "Midnight feedings? Diaper…?"

Her meaning registered in his sluggish brain and he froze in his tracks. "You mean…Are you…?" He couldn't seem to form a complete sentence. But then, with Lucy, he didn't need to.

Her grin widened and she nodded her head. "We're going to have a baby," she confirmed.

With a loud whoop, he wrapped his arms around her waist, lifted her off the ground and spun her in circles. Before they could get too dizzy, he set her back down, but didn't let go.

Through her laughter, she said, "I take it you're happy about this."

"Are you kidding? I'm ecstatic. I can't wait." He took a minute to catch his breath and then asked, "When?"

"Seven months. The doctor says early June."

"June. I'm gonna be a daddy in June," he breathed in wonder. And then he looked deep into her blue eyes. "I'll be a good one. I swear it."

"I know you will." Raising up on her toes, she held his cheeks in her cupped hands and kissed the corner of his mouth. "I've always known. You're a better man than you give yourself credit for, Peter Reynolds."

He swallowed past the lump of emotion clogging his throat. "I love you, Lucy Reynolds."

Leaning back in his arms, she smiled softly. "I know that, too."

* * * * *

**Welcome to Silhouette Desire's
brand-new installment of**

*The drama unfolds for six of
the state's wealthiest bachelors.*

BLACK-TIE SEDUCTION
by Cindy Gerard
(Silhouette Desire #1665, July 2005)

LESS-THAN-INNOCENT
INVITATION
by Shirley Rogers
(Silhouette Desire #1671, August 2005)

STRICTLY CONFIDENTIAL
ATTRACTION
by Brenda Jackson
(Silhouette Desire #1677, September 2005)

*Look for three more titles from Michelle Celmer,
Sara Orwig and Kristi Gold to follow.*

If you enjoyed what you just read,
then we've got an offer you can't resist!

Take 2 bestselling love stories FREE!

Plus get a FREE surprise gift!

Clip this page and mail it to Silhouette Reader Service™

IN U.S.A.
3010 Walden Ave.
P.O. Box 1867
Buffalo, N.Y. 14240-1867

IN CANADA
P.O. Box 609
Fort Erie, Ontario
L2A 5X3

YES! Please send me 2 free Silhouette Desire® novels and my free surprise gift. After receiving them, if I don't wish to receive anymore, I can return the shipping statement marked cancel. If I don't cancel, I will receive 6 brand-new novels every month, before they're available in stores! In the U.S.A., bill me at the bargain price of $3.80 plus 25¢ shipping and handling per book and applicable sales tax, if any*. In Canada, bill me at the bargain price of $4.47 plus 25¢ shipping and handling per book and applicable taxes**. That's the complete price and a savings of at least 10% off the cover prices—what a great deal! I understand that accepting the 2 free books and gift places me under no obligation ever to buy any books. I can always return a shipment and cancel at any time. Even if I never buy another book from Silhouette, the 2 free books and gift are mine to keep forever.

225 SDN DZ9F
326 SDN DZ9G

Name	(PLEASE PRINT)	
Address	Apt.#	
City	State/Prov.	Zip/Postal Code

Not valid to current Silhouette Desire® subscribers.

Want to try two free books from another series?
Call 1-800-873-8635 or visit www.morefreebooks.com.

* Terms and prices subject to change without notice. Sales tax applicable in N.Y.
** Canadian residents will be charged applicable provincial taxes and GST.
  All orders subject to approval. Offer limited to one per household.
  ® are registered trademarks owned and used by the trademark owner and or its licensee.

DES04R   ©2004 Harlequin Enterprises Limited

COMING NEXT MONTH

#1663 BETRAYED BIRTHRIGHT—Sheri WhiteFeather
Dynasties: The Ashtons
When Walker Ashton decided to search for his past, he found it on a
Sioux Nation reservation. Helping him to deal with his Native American
heritage was Tamra Winter Hawk, a woman who cherished her roots
and had Walker longing for a future together. But when his real-world
commitments intruded upon their fantasy liaison, would they find a way
to keep the connection they'd formed?

#1664 THE LAST REILLY STANDING—Maureen Child
Three-Way Wager
Aidan Reilly was determined to win the bet he'd made with his brothers.
Three months without sex meant one thing: spend *a lot* of time with his
best gal pal, Terry Evans. She had given up on love long ago because the
pain just wasn't worth it. Then…temptation proved to be too much. The last
Reilly standing had lost the bet, but could he win the girl?

#1665 BLACK-TIE SEDUCTION—Cindy Gerard
Texas Cattleman's Club: The Secret Diary
Millionaire Jacob Thorne got on Christine Travers's last nerve—the sensible
lady had no time for Jacob's flirtatious demeanor. But when the two butted
heads at an auction, Jacob embarked on a black-tie seduction that would
prove she had needs—womanly needs—that only he could satisfy.

#1666 THE RUGGED LONER—Bronwyn Jameson
Princes of the Outback
Australian widower Tomas Carlisle was stunned to learn he had to father
a child to inherit a cattle empire. Making a deal with longtime friend
Angelina Mori seemed the perfect solution—until their passion escalated
and Angelina mounted an all-out attack on Tomas's defense against hot,
passionate, *committed* love.

#1667 CRAVING BEAUTY—Nalini Singh
They'd married within mere days of meeting. Successful tycoon
Marc Bordeaux had been enchanted by Hira Dazirah's desert beauty. But
Hira feared Marc only craved her outer good looks. This forced Marc to
prove his true feelings to his virgin bride—and tender actions spoke louder
than words….

#1668 LIKE LIGHTNING—Charlene Sands
Although veterinarian Maddie Brooks convinced rancher Trey Walker to
allow her to live and work on his ranch, there was no way Trey would ever
romance the sweet and sexy Maddie. He was a victim of the "Walker Curse"
and couldn't commit to any woman. But once they gave in to temptation,
Maddie was determined to make their arrangement more permanent….

SDCNM0605

**Coming in July 2005
from Silhouette Desire**

DYNASTIES : THE ASHTONS

*A family built on lies...brought together
by dark, passionate secrets.*

Sheri WhiteFeather's
BETRAYED
BIRTHRIGHT

(Silhouette Desire #1663)

When Walker Ashton decided to search for his
past, he found it on a Sioux Nation reservation.
Helping him to deal with his Native American
heritage was Tamra Winter Hawk, a woman who
cherished her roots and had Walker longing
for a future with her. But when his real world
commitments intruded upon their fantasy
liaison, would they find a way to keep the
connection they'd formed?

Available at your favorite retail outlet.